The Virtual Life of Lexie Diamond

VICTORIA FOYT

HarperTempest
An Imprint of HarperCollinsPublishers

Quotation on p. 29 is from "The Love Song of J. Alfred Prufrock," © 1917 by T. S. Eliot, in *The Wasteland and Other Poems* (New York: Harcourt, Brace and World, 1934), page 3.

HarperTempest is an imprint of HarperCollins Publishers.
The Virtual Life of Lexie Diamond
Copyright © 2007 by Victoria Foyt

Library of Congress Cataloging-in-Publication Data
Foyt, Victoria.
    The virtual life of Lexie Diamond / Victoria Foyt. — 1st ed.
       p.   cm.
    Summary: Fourteen-year-old Lexie is at peace only while using her computer, so when her mother dies suddenly, Lexie tries to connect with her online and not only discovers that her mother was murdered, but learns that her father's new girlfriend is big trouble.
    ISBN-10: 0-06-082563-4 (trade bdg.)
    ISBN-13: 978-0-06-082563-8 (trade bdg.)
    ISBN-10: 0-06-082564-2 (lib. bdg.)
    ISBN-13: 978-0-06-082564-5 (lib. bdg.)
    [1. Interpersonal relations—Fiction. 2. Self-actualization (Psychology)—Fiction. 3. Supernatural—Fiction. 4. World Wide Web—Fiction. 5. Family life—California—Fiction. 6. Murder—Fiction. 7. Santa Monica (Calif.)—Fiction.] I. Title.
PZ7.F84124Vir 2007   2006029873
[Fic]—dc22   CIP
                                                             AC

Typography by Larissa Lawrynenko
1 2 3 4 5 6 7 8 9 10
❖
First Edition

To
Sabrina and Simon—
never forget
who you are.

ACKNOWLEDGMENTS

With a grateful heart I would like to thank
Henry Jaglom for a creative partnership in which my
own voice has always been recognized.

To Aram Saroyan for giving me the nod.

To Judith Searle for recognizing Lexie's voice.

To Catherine Ingram for her friendship.

To my agent, Linda Loewenthal, for her passion.

To the supportive staff at HarperCollins and to my
editor, Sally Doherty, for her insights and perseverance.

To my parents for their good example.

We have discovered the truth
and it makes no sense!
—G. K. CHESTERTON

LEXIE BEGAN HER Access Ritual in anticipation of entering realms of unimaginable freedom. With a light touch, she placed her index finger on the power button on her old Macintosh desktop computer, which she called "Ajna-Mac." Then she touched the spot in between her eyebrows—the ajna chakra point, or psychic opening, which was her computer's namesake. Three times, gently back and forth, Lexie touched the button and her forehead until she experienced the familiar, gradual detachment from the external world. She was entering the domain of pure thought, and her body seemed to float underneath her.

At last she turned the computer on, and as the green button on Ajna-Mac's hard drive shone as bright as a magic emerald crystal, she felt the addictive surge of energy run through her.

Lexie was Ajna-Mac's devoted disciple, and her worship began with the electronic sound of a simple prayer that invoked her master's presence—"Go ahead. Make my day!"

She went online, and as her modem rang out, she glanced at the three purple-haired Iggy dolls that were glued to the top of her computer and imagined them singing: *beep, la, bee-beep, la, la.* It was a sound that never failed to please Lexie—a chant to the e-gods: *Let me in, let me in, I belong on the Web!*

Only one thing distracted her: the gift sitting on her desk. The note on top read:

> *Congratulations, Madame President!*
> *I'm so proud of you.*
> *Love, Mom*

It had been a justifiable lie, Lexie reassured herself. For God's sake, her mother had threatened to restrict her computer time if she didn't improve her "social profile at school." At first Lexie had only told her she'd joined the computer club (in fact, she'd attended one meeting, during which she'd played video games by herself). But that had failed to please her mom—"Do they have virtual meetings?" Finally Lexie had had to amp up the lie: "Well, I'm president of the club—is that good enough?" Apparently it was. Beaming with pride, her mother had repeated Lexie's new title several times: President of the Virtual Club. Since the elections were still a few weeks away, however, Lexie feared her mother might see the campaign posters at school and bust her.

She understood that her mother, like all parents, hoped to control her by attacking the only thing that Lexie really cared about. It was a humiliating loop. In the beginning, parents would encourage you to get more and more involved in a hobby or sport, once they realized that you liked it or maybe even had some talent for it. They'd go out of their way to support this special interest (Lexie's mother had bought her tons of CD-ROMs). You thought these expressions of parental approval meant they truly understood that a sacred trust had been formed around the one thing that you could claim as your own in this unjust world into which you did not ask to be born. You were absolutely sure of this. And then one day—an unforgivable betrayal—your parents began to use it against you! Whenever that happened, you were entitled to lie, cheat, steal—whatever it took to protect it.

She slumped in her desk chair and opened the present. *A power booster!* She itched to load the high-capacity RAM chip into Ajna-Mac but held it in her hand for a moment, considering her options. If she kept it, she was obligated to make good on her lie. She would have no choice but to run for president of the Virtual Club. But Lexie would rather spend the rest of her miserable life locked in her room than run for public office. That would require dealing with people. The other choice was equally dismal: return the gift, confess, and suffer the disastrous consequences.

Before she could decide between two treacherous fates, her cell phone rang. MOM'S CELL. Lexie put the call on speakerphone.

At least she could surf the Web while they talked. Who knew how much longer she'd be free?

Her mother's soft voice filled the room. "Hi, sweetheart. I'm driving home."

Lexie mumbled something that passed for hello.

"Did you make any official decisions today, Miss President?" Her mother laughed to herself, and Lexie cringed.

"Um, no, no decisions," she said.

"Perhaps you'd like to invite the club members over for a party."

Lexie broke out in a cold sweat. "I think that's against the rules."

"Oh, pity. I guess it's not an egalitarian approach; not everyone can afford to throw a party."

"Yeah, not egalitarian." Lexie fingered the new booster, her conscience teetering back and forth.

"Show me the club handbook, sweetie. Perhaps I can come up with an idea or two."

Ugh! Lexie didn't want to be in a stupid club or spend any more of her precious energy lying about it, either! This was just another one of Earth's Alien Masters' sick jokes. She resented being trapped just because her poor mother was impressed by the illusory icons that they dangled in front of people's screens in order to distract them from the truth: *Earthlings lived in an unreal Bubble.*

It was a clever trick. Fixated on the screen of their lives and the enticing programs that ran on it—hip clothes, report cards, money, cool friends, club presidencies—average humans never even thought about the mechanics behind the whole system. But Lexie suspected that Peeping Tom aliens, amused by their cute little fishbowl humans, had long ago constructed a blue globe around this virtual world in order to prevent people from freaking out over their unreal, petlike existence. In fact, this Bubble was designed to make you forget that you were just an insignificant speck on a big dust ball spinning in the Milky Way among billions of galaxies.

Only online, traveling within the oneness of it all, did Lexie feel at peace with being just another icon inside some Great Geek's cosmic Game Boy. Any day now she expected to see the news posted online by physicists: Life as we knew it was fake, totally fake.

Once again she was forced to lie. "Um, webrider is sending me some tips on how to run a club," she said.

There was a warning tone in her mother's voice. "Honey, you're president of a club now. You can communicate with *real* people."

"Mom, webrider is, like, my best friend." How could her mom even say that? Webrider was real. They had been e-pals forever.

Her mother sidestepped the issue, and as she continued, Lexie listened with the peculiar awareness of a second, simulta-neous version of her mother speaking on what Lexie called the

Monitor B side of life. From an early age, she had sensed that things were seldom as they appeared to be. When people said things, they usually meant something else. If you paid close attention, you could almost perceive their shadows, like puppets, right behind them, acting out what they were really saying. For example, at this moment:

Mom, Monitor A: "I always knew that if you wanted to expand out of your private world, you could easily extend yourself. And how wonderful that this club presidency, which represents a shift in your socialization skills, is occurring at such a pivotal point in your development."

Mom's Shadow, Monitor B: *You're not the daughter I thought I'd have, but if you will cooperate, I will work hard to make you more acceptable.*

On Monitor A, life played, and on Monitor B, its subtext.

Sometimes Lexie even wished she could have been as Bubble-happy as a cheerleader, comfortable in a Monitor A world, never seeing Monitor B. After all, it was exhausting having to compare the two sides. And once she became aware of the person's true meaning, she found it hard, if not impossible, to play along with the A version. Which was probably why she had no offline friends.

Upset by her mom's comments, Lexie considered exposing her mom's B-meaning. Experience had taught her, however, that her mother would simply deny it. In fact, the more well adjusted the pet was, the bigger the denial. She would insist her praise

6

was heartfelt, while Lexie knew she was only transmitting Bubble logic. Lexie was caught, therefore, in the dead space between the two monitors, which always had a numbing effect on her.

To make matters worse, her mother said, "I was wondering if webrider is a girlfriend or"—her voice rose with a glimmer of embarrassing hope—"a boyfriend?"

Lexie stared at Ajna-Mac's screen, and for the first time, it occurred to her that she didn't know. Ever since that memorable moment three years ago when she and webrider had discussed the ARPANET, the first version of the Internet, in a chat room for gearheads, they had been inseparable. She scanned through their e-history but found no gender labeling on either side. Of course, why would it matter to Lexie? Online everyone was just, like, energy.

But the difference seemed vital to her mother. Lexie's Internal Screen split: on one side it read GIRL; across from it, BOY. Countless possible future projections based on past parental encounters scrolled down each side. With a quick analysis, Lexie understood her mother's underlying concern. No boyfriends meant that Lexie had not secured a firm foothold on the evolutionary ladder that next led to marriage, a home loan, grandchildren, and her contribution to the continuing spiral of so-called happiness within the Bubble.

"Boy," Lexie said. Besides, with a 50 percent chance of being right, technically it wasn't a lie, was it?

"That's nice, sweetie," her mother said. Having gotten a glimpse of Lexie as a well-behaved resident of the Bubble, however, she spoke with increased passion. "But don't forget, I'm talking about having real communication, talking to people and listening to what they say."

Lexie retaliated. "Like you and Dad do?"

There was a pause on the other end of the line. As a kid, Lexie had been encouraged by her mother to express her feelings. But as her mother backspaced away from the question, Lexie wondered if there was an age limit to "open communication."

"Your father and I talk," her mother said at last.

Just then, a second call came through. Lexie smirked at the irony: DAD-WORK.

Lexie hesitated, but her mom prompted her. "Who's calling?" she said.

"Dad."

"Put him on."

"I'll call him back."

"Lexie, it's all right. Put him on."

"Whatever." She hooked up his call, and her father's voice boomed out in the room.

"Hi, honey! How are you, diamondstar?" he said, addressing Lexie by her screen name.

"Hi, Dad." Her voice uncontrollably morphed into a nondistinct, jellyfish version of itself. She wasn't quite sure where she stood with him, but she knew it was on slippery ground. She couldn't say why, but the change had started a year ago on her thirteenth birthday, and then when the divorce followed soon afterward, he had virtually disappeared.

"How's school?" her father said. "I haven't heard from you in a while."

"It's okay," Lexie said.

"You know, David, if you showed up more, you'd know how things were," Lexie's mother said.

"Oh. Hi, Grace. We're on a three-way, Lexie?"

"Uh-huh." Then, as usual, her parents ignored her and went into Fight Mode.

"I've been working very hard, Grace—"

"But you promised that we would—"

"What's the point? You—"

"Well maybe if *you'd* listen—"

"*You're* the one who isn't listening!"

Lexie stared up at the mobile twirling from the ceiling above her desk in the evening breeze. She had made it years ago with metal springs and silicon chips, and now, as the silvery pieces chased after one another, it reminded her of her parents. Why couldn't they see that they were always spinning in circles? Mesmerized by the mobile's swirling movement, Lexie suddenly found herself propelled toward the center of her mind, where her *Internal Graphics* program was activated.

After spending countless hours online with Ajna-Mac and

many hundreds of dollars on video games, Lexie had naturally developed the ability to program mental images that were as refined, even as 3-D, to Lexie as those pictures that the rest of the world called "real life." This skill was especially comforting to Lexie during high-stress situations. Like when her parents were fighting.

I'm sitting at my desk when suddenly, from somewhere in the strato-sphere, I hear a loud Pop! *I run to the window and see the whole sky— clouds, moon, and stars—being sucked up into a black hole with a loud slurping sound. The Bubble-pricker peers over the edge of this heavenly crater, looking down into our rapidly disappearing world. Caught up in the suction, I effortlessly float out of my house. I'm falling into the abyss when I remember that I haven't said good-bye to my parents.*

She considered hanging up on her parents when a loud beep from Ajna-Mac interrupted her gloomy thoughts. She was struck by AOL's Message of the Day, which seemed to go 3-D on her: BELIEVE IN YOUR OWN POWER. But what power did she have in this screwed-up Bubble?

A second beep from her e-guru, however, along with her own nagging feeling that she should do *something* to help her battling parents, encouraged her. Once again she laid her finger on Ajna-Mac's power button while pressing the point between her eyebrows with another finger. She closed her eyes and, with great intention, said to herself, *I call forth the truth, and the power of the Web, and I now decree that my parents learn to listen!* When she opened her eyes a large black spider dropped down its silken thread in front of the screen. *Yuck!*

She captured the invading creature inside an empty CD case, ran over to the window and—as if ridding her life of all its uncertainty—shook the case until the spider dropped two floors onto the bushes below. A cold shiver went up her spine, and she wondered if its icky presence had contaminated her wish.

Indeed, her parents' argument reached a crescendo. She shot a knowing look at her computer. *See? I told you it was no use.*

At least she didn't have to listen anymore to their childish conversation. She grabbed the cell phone to turn it off when a horrible *BANG!* stung her ears. She heard her mother scream her name, *"LEXIE!"* Before she could respond, the line went dead. Lexie's gut lurched, and as if mirroring her turmoil, her computer ground out an agonizing metallic glitch, followed by a sharp, startling *PING!* sound. The screen darkened, and she realized he had shut down.

Lexie banged on Ajna-Mac's power button, which seemed frozen in terror. *What's going on?*

For once, he didn't answer.

THE HOT WHITE glare of late afternoon seeped between Lexie's black curtains, and she squinted her eyes, scanning her purple bedroom. Everything looked the same, but life as she knew it had ended the night before. She closed her eyes once more and, just in case she had been dreaming, tempted fate with, "Mom?" She knew no answer would come, but her mother's absence seemed so unreal. Just yesterday morning, they had been together in the kitchen. She had kissed Lexie on the top of her head. Wouldn't she kiss her anymore? Tears welled up in Lexie's eyes. Mom said she would be at the office. *Be at the office,* Lexie repeated to herself, trying to grasp the idea that her mother *wasn't* at the office, or anywhere. She was gone forever. It didn't seem possible.

Lexie recalled her mother standing in the doorway, briefcase in hand, surrounded by the soft morning light. "Bye. I love you, Shiny Diamond," she'd said, just like on every other morning. Those words connected them with an invisible strength, woven like steel over the years. Lexie had always counted on her mother being there. Had Lexie even told her mother that she loved her, too? She'd probably muttered some monosyllabic response. But Mom understood, didn't she? Lexie sighed—she wasn't sure.

With sudden horror, she recalled their last conversation and was overwhelmed with guilt about the lies she had told. If only she could hit Rewind and play over their last moments. But life on Earth wasn't as sophisticated as even the simplest video game. Instead one random moment could permanently change your whole life. There was no control, no stability when you lived at the whim of some Pet Master's moods.

Her father walked in her room, as if stepping on eggshells. "Hi, honey. Are you all right?" he said.

She nodded vaguely, with both a dip and a turn of the head, a sort of yes/no. She had long ago learned it left her options open.

"Come to the kitchen. I made some food."

"I'm not hungry." She turned to face the wall.

"Lexie, please, you have to eat something. If you don't come downstairs, I'll bring food to your room. Either way, you're going to eat. Okay?"

"Whatever," she said as he left.

She rolled out of bed, surprised to find herself wearing yesterday's clothes, and padded over to her computer. "Rough night, huh, Ajna-Mac?" she said as she began her Access Ritual. She hoped he'd recovered his balance, because if ever she needed a virtual reality infusion, it was now. To her great relief, Ajna-Mac opened his arms to receive her, and she soon sailed into the great wide Web.

Here, in Lexie's playground, she could forget about the vagaries of the Bubble for a while. Just like other kids, she had developed street smarts on her turf, too. She had learned to decipher all there was to know about someone from their cyberchat style. No one had taught her. Telltale clues were simply obvious to her: a person's netiquette; how geekspeaky a message sounded; how long someone's net-lag took; if there was any poetry or bragging in the screen name; if a person hogged the space or made room for the next user; and, most important of all, if that person understood why they were online. In her mind, those that did formed an elite surfing group; they didn't need wet suits.

Sometimes, as she surfed the waves of the Web, she thought of herself as a musician picking up the beat. It wasn't just lines of banal conversation thrown out into some abysmal, freewheeling, atmospheric junk pit. No, this was great jazz. There was rhyme and reason to it. There was syncopation. When she was in really top form, she became one with the beat. Then, with total abandon, her fingers danced across her keyboard to

14

the pulse of the universe. Oh, it was heaven. She often wondered if sex would be as good.

Comforted by a few stops at her favorite haunts, she found the courage to visit Lincoln Middle School's Virtual Club address. At least she would attempt to cancel the lies she'd told her mom. She e-mailed a request to the computer teacher:

please add my name to the ballot for the virtual
club presidency.
thanks,
lexie diamond

She was sure to win; none of the other gearheads would care enough to run for office. It was a small price to pay for having lied to her mom. Anyway, she couldn't afford any more bad karma.

Karma basically meant that when you did something bad or good, something similar would eventually happen back to you, maybe this lifetime, maybe next. It had nothing to do with your astrological sign, either. According to karmic theory your scorecard began whenever your particular energy was first created, probably many lifetimes ago. Since the law of physics dictated that energy could not be destroyed, only transformed, Lexie figured karma made sense. She also figured her scorecard was in the danger zone by now. Pretty soon she would have to do something really cool like helping to save the rain forest; otherwise Karma Kong, Lexie's idea of life's ultimate scorekeeper—a righteous, all-knowing ape who kept track of her actions—

might stomp on her screen and shut her down for good.

Hoping she'd adjusted her karmic balance, she decided there was no point in returning the power booster her mother had given her. As she loaded it into her computer's motherboard, Ajna-Mac emitted the tinkling e-laugh he made whenever Lexie tickled his insides. At once she felt her spirits lift. She jumped back online and soon found herself soaring around the Web with incredible new velocity. Until Lexie accessed a site, it lay in some universal amniotic bath, floating unseen, inactive, waiting for her command to spring to life. Now, supercharged, she felt empowered to access the outer limits of cyberspace. Technology was so predictable, so pure. If only life were that elegant.

"You've got mail," her e-postman announced.

webrider. Her habit was to read e-mails aloud—it made her feel less lonely.

> hey, whassup, diamondstar? catch this tune. kinda
> moody. made me think of you.

Lexie smiled; somewhere out there in the Web was someone who understood her. She had told her mom that webrider was a boy, but staring at the familiar style of communication—all lowercase, lots of abbreviations, no greeting or sign-off (there was no time to be polite when there were so many cyberwaves to catch)—Lexie realized that, in the back of her mind, she had always thought of her friend as a girl, just like herself. Cybertwins, in fact. To ask for a gender label now, after all these years of intimate e-chats, would be ridiculous.

She downloaded the song and, as the music filled her room, typed her reply:

hey, cool music. thanks.

Then with the objectivity of a reporter, she laid out the facts and hit Send:

my mom died in a car accident yesterday. i'm a
half-orphan now.

The response was swift, and classic webrider with its positive spin:

wow. sorry. don't worry, i'm here for you. 4ever.

But nothing was forever, was it? They were all tethered to the Bubble, until some Alien in Charge decided they weren't. *Pfft!* Gone. Just like that.

Her father yelled from downstairs, interrupting her dismal thoughts. "Lexie, are you coming down?"

"Yeah," she said, not caring whether or not he heard her.

She would have preferred to stay in the sanctuary of her cave for the rest of time, but she needed to refuel, and she sure didn't want her dad violating her space again. She logged off. Webrider would understand there was only one person she wanted to talk to: *Mom.*

She shuffled down the stairs through what now felt like foreign territory and went into the kitchen. Her father gave her a plastic smile as she slumped into her chair at the table. Lexie stabbed at the watery scrambled eggs he placed in front of her, and they ate in silence like two robotic automatons, moving without sensory input.

Weighted down by my space suit, I walk through the burning field of a supernova. I see someone meandering ahead. I approach him and peer curiously into his helmet. My scanner output reads: YOUR FATHER. *I'm sure he is from my home planet, but I don't recognize him.*

"I promise, we'll get through this," her father said at last.

But she had lost faith in his promises. She nodded in that half-question/half-answer way of hers, wondering why they weren't pals anymore. Her Internal Memory clicked open the file MISSING DAD, and she remembered the echo of her young voice yelling "Daaaddy!" whenever he came home. That dad had seemed more interested in her, and sometimes she wanted him back. Wasn't she still the same Lexie, only older? Maybe life had changed; maybe it was more accessible in the old days. Her parents had been less remote then. After all, it was her dad who had introduced her to the Web; he had given her Ajna-Mac.

Then she pulled up FIRST TIME ONLINE. She had been totally psyched. Even now, she could remember the same giddy feeling that had run through her six-year-old body on that first visit to the computer store. The minute she spied the gray Macintosh Power PC, her heart had done a little somersault; she had to have it. Her father had pressed his index finger between her eyebrows and said in his serious, I'm-teaching-you-a-lesson-now tone, "In India they have a word for the point of your body through which you can see the future. If you strive to develop this center, called the third eye or ajna"—he rounded out the syllables slowly, making her repeat after him: *ahj-nah*—"you can use your mind to achieve great success." She had wanted to tell him: I'm only in kindergarten, I don't want to be successful, I just want a computer. But he had looked so pleased that she had hugged him instead. Still, she thought the whole Indian thing sounded cool, so she had dubbed her computer "Ajna-Mac."

The doorbell rang, startling Lexie and her father. "Are you expecting anyone?" he said.

Lexie rolled her eyes. *Duh? Who would visit me?* Her father nodded, as if remembering who she was, and went to answer the door.

"Mr. Diamond?" A strange, abrasive audio floated in from the foyer.

"Yes?" her father said.

"I'm Detective Blackwell. I need to ask a few questions about Mrs. Diamond if that's all right with you?"

Lexie peered down the hall and saw a big man standing in the doorway. His presence brought certainty that her mom was really gone, and Lexie hated him for it.

"Of course," her father replied as he led the plainclothes cop into the kitchen. He gestured to her. "This is my daughter." Blackwell coughed, his throat rattling with a smoker's death sentence, and stole an uncomfortable glance at her.

But she would not be ignored. "What happened to my mother?" she asked him.

In his nicotine-stained fingers he held a bracelet of small wooden beads, continually sliding the beads in one direction. Obviously he was using these worry beads to kick his gross cigarette habit. His fingers slowed, and he trained his deep dark eyes on Lexie, as if he was really seeing her now. *Are these beads some new kind of B-speak?* she wondered. He softened his voice too, talking slower than normal, in Adult Speak, which grown-ups used whenever they had to deal with kids.

"I'm sorry, miss," he said. "Right now we believe it was an accidental hit-and-run."

Like mother, like daughter, thought Lexie, who figured her own arrival in the Bubble had been an accident. With a stoic gaze she stared at the detective, encouraging him to continue. But he focused his attention once more on her father. Predictably, his voice resumed its artillerylike, staccato rhythm.

"It appears that a heavy vehicle crossed your wife's lane," he said. "The perpetrator seems to have driven off quickly. Unfortunately it was dark, and there were no witnesses. Was there anything unusual about her driving home at eight thirty on a Thursday?"

"Grace was a psychiatrist," Lexie's father said. "She used to work late on Thursdays. Had that changed, Lexie?"

Blackwell's eyebrows arched. "Don't you live here?"

"We divorced last year."

"I see." Blackwell leveled his gaze at Lexie once more. "Anything unusual about your mother coming home at that hour?"

Lexie shook her head in her ambiguous way.

"Was that a no?" he said.

She shuffled her feet impatiently and finally said, "No."

"Do you mean no it wasn't a no, or no she didn't work late on Thursdays?"

Lexie rolled her eyes. Communication on this planet was as convoluted as life itself. Mirroring his Adult Speak, she spoke with slow emphasis. "My mom always works late on Thursdays."

Blackwell paused, moving the beads to write on a small pad, and then continued. "Mrs. Diamond was driving within the speed limit north along Ocean Avenue. The accident occurred about a mile from here, near the intersection with Idaho. Does that strike you as odd?"

"That's her route," Lexie said. Her mother's life was as predictable as their conversations.

For the first time a bit of human warmth crept into Blackwell's voice. "When did you last see your mother, miss?"

"Yesterday morning," Lexie said, never taking her eyes from the floor.

"And how did she seem?" he said, stretching out the last word, as if to imply that the word *seem* could mean more than "seem"--that it meant everything that existed underneath what "seemed."

How did she seem? It was just a question, but it unplugged Lexie's whole system, and she got lost in a storm of fragmented thoughts: like Mom deserved more. Like she wanted to be just a little bit happier in this godforsaken Bubble. Like Lexie should have been nicer to her when she had the chance. Like a really cool person that she hardly got to know. Like someone Lexie loved more than anything in the whole world.

A great, big ball of grief was moving through Lexie; it started at the tips of her toes and rolled heavily up her body. If she let it crush her, she knew she would never stop crying. She summoned all her willpower and braced herself against it, holding it just one tear away from total devastation. Her voice cracked when she finally answered Blackwell.

"She seemed fine."

"Did she say anything unusual to you, anything at all?"

"Just what she always says."

Said, Lexie corrected herself. *Mom always said.* Oh God, how could she use the past tense for her mother? With this small adjustment, the reality of her new life began to sink in.

"And what's that?"

Lexie slowly recited her mom's words. " 'You know how to reach me if you need me.' " If only Lexie could. Until now, it had been a constant, not a variable. Her mother had always been a phone call away.

Blackwell gave a dismissive nod and continued. "Was your

22

mother upset lately, for any reason?"

Lexie stared in silent accusation at her father, and Blackwell gunned his eyes on him in turn.

"Are you remarried, Mr. Diamond?"

"No, single."

"When did you last see your ex-wife?"

"I can't remember, exactly—maybe a month ago."

"And when did you last speak to her?"

Lexie's father's deep sigh cleaved the tension in the room. "Yesterday, on the cell phone, at the time of the accident," he said.

"And how would you describe your conversation?"

With an apologetic look at Lexie, her father appeared to contract as he confessed: "We were having an argument."

Blackwell shook his head in dismay and jotted something on his notepad. "I see it all the time," he said after a long moment. "Someone's arguing on the cell phone instead of paying attention to the road. I wish the damn things were illegal in California."

Dad's fault? If he had never left them, then her mother might still be there. It was as if a bomb detonated inside of Lexie's heart, shattering its already fragile state into jagged shards.

"One more thing," Blackwell said, referring to his notes. "We found an abandoned vehicle a mile away that might have been involved. It's registered to a John Simpson. Either of you know someone by that name?"

Lexie gave him a blank stare, and her father said, "No, we don't know him."

"Okay, folks," he said, still nervously clicking the irritating beads. "Thanks for your time."

Draining her last energy reserves, she activated her backup disks and managed to eject her floppy self from the kitchen. She stumbled up the stairs into her room and slammed the door shut behind her. Sobbing, she collapsed next to Ajna-Mac. If only, she wished, a giant meteor would collide with Earth right then and delete the whole stupid Bubble, once and for all. A minute later, her father knocked on her door.

"Lexie, please . . ."

"Go away!" she said.

He pleaded with her to open the door, but she ignored him. "All right," he called out. "Let's talk later. I'll be right across the hall, if you need me."

In a flash, she was on her feet. She ran across the room and flung open the door.

"You can't stay in Mom's room!"

"Why not? It's my old room."

"Because, you just can't! Mom doesn't want you to, and neither do I."

"Lexie, I'm not leaving."

"Then stay in the guest room."

For a moment he looked stunned, as if she had slapped him.

Lexie felt the urge to reach out and hug him, only she couldn't. An invisible but impenetrable wall had split them apart into separate universes. She would never forgive him. She closed the door in his face.

As she roved from one end of her room to the other, back and forth, with no aim but to keep moving, some deep part of Lexie was aware that she was no longer driving her own body. But she no longer cared who was pushing her personal mouse around the disintegrating pad of her mind.

Glancing up at a bulletin board over her desk filled with photos, stickers, ticket stubs, and a few of her M. C. Escher–inspired pencil drawings, she felt drawn to a digital photo of her mother taken in Maui on their last family summer vacation. Lexie had always liked that photo, only it felt lopsided to Lexie now; the whole world was at a tilt. If only she could shimmy up to the top and bungee-jump off into Nothingness. She peered into the image, wishing that she could reach beyond it to the past and hear her mother's voice one more time.

Suddenly, realizing that she *could*, she grabbed a DVD labeled MAUI, SUMMER VACATION from her bookshelf. Her parents had given her a digital camcorder as a present, hoping, she suspected, to lure her outdoors. In fact, during their trip Lexie had followed her parents around, recording their every word, until they had seemed relieved when she had disappeared as usual into her room back at home.

She inserted the DVD into Ajna-Mac's disc drive, and as if the home movie held some magic power, hit Play with a reverent touch. A little gasp of pleasure escaped Lexie's lips as her mother appeared on the computer screen, full of life. She was walking on the beach with her back to the camera.

There was Mom. *See, she's not dead.* It only confirmed Lexie's belief when her mother turned around at that moment and smiled.

"Oh, Lexie, I'm wearing a bathing suit!" she said, frowning with displeasure at the camera.

Lexie's disembodied voice could be heard: "So what?" she said. "You look great."

She had never understood her mother's obsession with her figure. She had never looked fat to Lexie. And seeing her in the home movie, she confirmed that her mother looked great. But despite her mother's willowy size six, Lexie had had to endure her mother's endless progression from one diet to the next. Each time, her mother would decide that Lexie should also benefit from the wisdom that she was now gaining from her latest nutritional guru, especially since Lexie was "blossoming into a young lady," as her mother had often said. *Blossoming* being the key word. At fourteen years old, Lexie was already one dress size bigger than her mother and still growing. As usual Lexie had conflicting responses to her mother's help: On the one hand she wished her mother didn't care about Lexie's figure, and yet she secretly appreciated her mom's attention.

So she went along with her mother's dietary experiments,

although their opposite attitudes regarding food highlighted another fundamental difference in their design. Lexie saw herself as a simple machine that needed plain fuel, any kind of fuel, in order to operate. It didn't matter whether it was homemade pumpkin ravioli or candy bars. If she could have taken three pills a day in order to satisfy her caloric requirements, that would have been fine with her. For her mother, however, it seemed as if food was an enemy with which she was locked in a never-ending battle. On this point, Lexie knew that she and the aliens monitoring earthlings viewed her mother in the same strange way.

"I used to be in such great shape," her mother said on the screen.

"Before you had me, right?" Lexie said.

"Yeah." Her mother smiled, looking right into Lexie's camera. "And you were worth it. I'm a lucky mom."

Even through the screen, Lexie could feel the warmth of her mother's smile wrap around her trembling shoulders. There was no B-context at all in her mother's expression, only love.

Softly, Lexie said, "I love you, Mom."

But of course there was no response. Lexie sighed. She'd do anything for just one more minute together.

AS LEXIE'S FATHER drove her on the 405 freeway toward the cemetery in Culver City, her fingers tightened around a poetry book in her lap. It was late September and the Santa Ana winds blew hot and dry, setting people's nerves on edge.

Lexie glanced down at the copy of T. S. Eliot's *Collected Poems* several times, finding comfort in the stained, torn cover and dog-eared pages. It felt crushed with adoration like an old stuffed animal with bald patches.

"Mom really likes this book," she said, avoiding the past tense.

Her father nodded. "Yep, it was her favorite."

They drove in silence the rest of the way, though he glanced at her often from the corner of his eye. She didn't expect any further conversation or understanding from him. They were out of practice as friends, and neither seemed to know how to begin again. She stared out the car window, trying to pretend it was just another day.

Too soon, the guard directed them through Hillside Memorial's tall black gates, and Lexie was stunned to find herself at the grave site. As she listened to her grandfather read aloud the words that his daughter had treasured, his voice halting, then tumbling, like a little kid learning to walk, she longed to tell him how absurd this ritual was. Her mother was *not* dead.

". . . Oh, do not ask, 'What is it?' / Let us go and make our visit. / In the room the women come and go / Talking of Michelangelo." He paused to clear his throat and then continued.

Poor Poppa. He didn't understand. None of them did, Lexie thought as she surveyed the solemn faces of friends and relatives, all of whom were staring at the casket with the proper amount of respect and sadness. There wasn't even a glimmer of awareness, or any questioning thought on a single face. Was she the only one who thought this was a bad joke?

But she couldn't fight the weight of all their grief. To escape, she closed her eyes and drifted in her mind to her secret place. The graphics of Lexie's virtual hideaway were so vivid on her Internal Screen, having been tweaked a million times, that all she had to do was activate the roaring sound of the waterfall and it took her right there.

I'm far away from any sign of civilization, on a high mountaintop near a calm pool surrounded by weeping willows. The running water sings to me before beginning its dizzy descent into a chasm so deep that I can't see the river below, only the rising mist. I lie down under the trees and feel the cool grass against my skin. As the sun sets, it slips between the steep mountain inclines, coloring my retreat a fiery red-orange. I wish I could stay here forever.

With dual awareness she watched her mother's casket being lowered into the freshly turned ground. In that moment she realized exactly how crazy life on Earth truly was. Lexie no more believed that her mother was in that box than she believed that earthlings were the only form of intelligent life in the universe. This funereal mockery was the most obvious sign yet that the world was just an illusion: Reality was a shaky business.

Even now Lexie could feel her mother nearby. In fact, in the past few days since her mother had left, Lexie had had a growing awareness of her unmistakable presence. Just that morning, as Lexie had slipped her one and only dress over her head, she'd heard her mother's voice behind her. She'd turned, convinced that she would see her again. She hadn't, but that didn't prove her mother wasn't alive—Lexie had felt her!

Only humans were so fixated on their external, shell-like identities that they needed funerals. Superior beings probably recycled their body parts. Of course that would occur only after the Body Makers confirmed that the resident spirit had downloaded all of its reusable energy. Only then would the person's energy be merged with the latest equipment. They probably even had special Memory Banks where you could retrieve your long-term disks. Once you had restarted your identity, you could jump right back into your favorite chat rooms with the same username. No loss of connection at all. Even better, you could access your old ATM card and credit cards and stuff. And, of course, you'd always recognize your real mother, the one you had started from long ago. The path of Internal Identification was way superior to, although less popular than, Earth's current body-driven standard.

Sometimes it was so stressful holding a singular view of life. If only she could have talked to some higher intelligence, like an Intergalactic Big Sister.

A hush fell over the crowd as the poem ended. Lexie's grandmother took her by the hand and led her away. She looked up into Oma's tired green eyes, the same bright shade as Lexie's mother's, searching for some sign that she knew, or at least suspected, how ridiculous the burial had been. Her grandmother squeezed her hand tightly and smiled. It was a reassuring smile, and although it was only a copy, it reminded her of the one she loved best from her mother. Oma, she suspected, would understand. After all, she was cool.

A long time ago Lexie had realized that if her grandmother had been born fifty years later she would have been a geek, which was a major compliment in her opinion. Even though her

31

wiring was Jurassic, it was really elegant. She leaned her body against Oma's soft, loose warmth and caught the scent of the wintergreen Life Savers that she knew her grandmother would have tucked away in her purse. She was as addicted to them as Lexie's mother had been. Lexie held out her hand, and her grandmother, understanding their signal, dug out the familiar candy roll and handed her one.

Comforted, Lexie plunged into the essence of her dilemma. "Oma, what do you do when you really want to talk to someone and you can't reach them?"

"I suppose, dear . . ." Her grandmother paused, as if searching for an answer. "You have to remember the love you shared and that you'll always feel for that person."

"And then what?"

She squeezed Lexie's hand. "Then, as hard as it might seem, we have to learn to adjust to a different life."

Since Lexie was so plugged into patterns and sequences, she couldn't avoid the one her grandmother had just presented. Up to now, she hadn't really considered that she might never make it back to home page. If it had been her father speaking, she would have immediately deleted his advice. But the channel to her grandmother was wide open, and the data had already slipped through. She shuddered as Oma's words bounced around inside her heart, like metal balls hitting their pop-up, pinball targets. *A . . .* Ping! *. . . different . . .* Ping! *. . . life.*

"How do I do that?" Lexie said.

"Well, what do you think your mother would want you to do?"

Lexie tried to control her thoughts, but they were slipping like a Slinky going down stairs. She just hoped that when she reached bottom she would land with all her coils piled neatly on top of one another, not all twisted up.

At last a single, sure thought formed in her mind. "If I could only talk to Mom, I'd know what to do."

"Then by all means, talk to her," her grandmother said, as if the problem were easily solved. "Believe me, she's listening. I'm sure she'll answer you."

This was such a rad, major statement of consciousness that Lexie's mind reeled from the implications.

"Really?" she said.

Her grandmother smiled. "My dear Lexie, as sure as the sun shines, love never dies."

Lexie sure hoped so. But at home with her father once more, amid the silence and the debris of her past life, she found it hard to believe.

He fished a condolence card from a basket of flowers, and as Lexie watched him read it, she was disturbed by this primitive ritual. She was sure Earth's Masters would never stick dead flowers in a useless basket, write some gobbledygook on a piece of paper they'd gotten by terminating a living tree, and then send it to the grieving family. Any highly evolved being receiving this absurdity would surely blow the sender away for making a mockery of his pain.

Her father tucked the card back into the ridiculous basket, and then, without warning, he said, "Detective Blackwell called. They found the driver of the car. It was John Simpson's girlfriend. He had lent her his car." He drew in a deep breath. "She'd been drinking; she had a history of drunk driving."

"Had?" Lexie said.

"She killed herself. She left a confession note. The case is closed." He stared at her, perhaps expecting a response.

What did it matter? A random particle had ruined their lives. That was life in the Bubble.

THE HOT, DRY WINDS abated, and there was a hint of fall in the morning air. But the change in temperature did little to relieve Lexie's anxiety. She stood at her street corner for the first time in two weeks, trying to look like she didn't care that she was standing out in the open where everyone could examine her—not that anyone on the school bus would notice her. She knew that as far as they were concerned she was invisible.

A loud crack in the air told Lexie that her next-door neighbor, Wilson Wyler, had tumbled through the porch door of his bungalow-style house. She could easily picture him loping down the sidewalk: T-shirt on backward, long board shorts, and the untied shoelaces to his Converse high-tops following him like a tangle of faithful puppies. She could hear him approaching, followed by a scraping noise, which she guessed was his backpack being dragged on the ground. Her body tensed as he drew closer, although she knew they wouldn't speak—surfer dudes and gearheads were totally incompatible.

She glanced at him out of the corner of her eye, and to her horror, caught him checking her out on the sly. They both immediately looked away, as embarrassed as if they'd been found naked. Lexie wasn't sure why Wilson made her so self-conscious. He was cute enough with his long blond hair hanging over his bored eyes, but his brain, she figured, had long ago been baked in all that sunlight and saltwater. Unless her programming interfaced with some guy's, she doubted she would be attracted, no matter how cute he was. And Wilson just seemed too happy living in the Bubble.

As the bus slowed to a stop in front of them, he came within inches of her and mumbled something unintelligible, perhaps, "Hey." A curious, intense heat flashed through her, and she hoped her Internal Firewall would prevent her from having a meltdown in front of the whole world. She filed the strange incident under RANDOM EVENTS. Maybe a cosmic shift was occurring. Somehow she managed to mutter a similar greeting and follow him onto the bus. Her Karma Kong reminder—a little black ape attached to a key chain on her backpack—swung as she bounced up the steps.

At once she spied the leg-swinging, gum-chewing, hair-tossing cluster of girls through which she would have to pass. She could

oblivious to people's intentions, made way for the Blond Bomb.

Deal with it, diamondstar! Lexie told herself.

"Hi. I'm Zoe Lushing, your *president*," Zoe said in an irritating, singsong voice, enunciating each syllable of her title.

"I know," Lexie said, rolling her eyes.

Since Lexie knew that Zoe knew that *everyone* already knew who she was, she assumed that Zoe had only wanted to hear the sound of her new title. Until then, Zoe had just been a bleep on Lexie's scanner, mushed in with all the other Facsimile Girls. But now, face-to-face with this poseur, she realized that her deep instinct to ignore those poseurs had been totally right. She hated Zoe.

"I should be in charge of this club," Lexie said. In an unconscious, primitive attempt to mark her territory, she stretched her baggy T-shirt tight against embryonic breasts and pushed her pitiful chest into the air. But Zoe's breasts were bigger, at least a C cup already, and she didn't even take up the challenge.

With an amused grin on her acne-free face, she simply said, "Whatever. You can be, like, the *virtual* president. You didn't think I was going to do all the work, did you?"

Unaccustomed to battling with a real goddess, Lexie nearly toppled over at Zoe's lack of resistance to her puffed-up posturing. Since she had never thought of herself as a girl or a boy— just a terminal—the proximity of this much girl-power was overwhelming.

She locked her knees tight, trying to steady herself. "Why can't you just be a cheerleader? You're already dressed like one."

Zoe looked her up and down with a cool appraisal that made Lexie quiver. "As if," Zoe said. "That's not going to get me into Harvard. Computer science majors have a seventy-two percent higher chance of admission than liberal arts majors. You have to build your image now."

Image? What image? Lexie wondered. She didn't want an image. Was this really happening to her? Perhaps she was only watching a 3-D actualization of her fears. She closed her eyes briefly. No, Zoe was still there, tapping her pointed toe impatiently.

Okay, Lexie decided, the aliens in charge of her sector were playing a nasty trick on her. They had copied her worst nightmare onto a disk that was now being downloaded right into school. She was "it" today and she would just have to wait until the Masters of the Universe tired of toying with her.

Zoe pulled a scary-looking, spiked hairbrush out of her purse and began flipping it through her hair with professional finesse. Lexie had already observed her doing this dozens of times, and by now she understood that with Zoe's expert wrist action and the direction and speed of the hair tool, she was signaling Lexie in a kind of Barbiespeak. Slow long pulls, which traveled all the way to her trimmed ends, back to the center part and then, calmly, all the way down again meant "I'm waiting for you to acknowledge my power over you." Rapid, short strokes:

"You're boring me!" Now Zoe's brush was rapping out a hypnotic beat, as if it were a golden wand with the power to fulfill her every wish. Even Wilson, Lexie noticed in disgust, was mesmerized by Zoe's hair flips.

"I'll bet you've never even been online in your life!" Lexie said, feeling like a small kid flailing her arms in the empty space between her and the bully holding her back with an effortless, outstretched arm.

Zoe grinned. "You're right." Then she put her brush away and closed her purse with a loud snap, as if to say, Time's up! "You didn't actually think anyone would choose you, did you?" she said in mock amazement. "You're such a nerd, everyone thinks you're a mute."

Whoa, that was cold, Lexie thought. She was both intrigued and horrified by her rival's lack of B-filtering.

Just then, a group of Zoe's fans pushed past Lexie as if she didn't exist, reminding Lexie how invisible she was. With loud voices, several groupies asked The Starlet why she was hanging out "over here." Of course, Lexie understood that they were interviewing Zoe the way any human group would if one of their kind experienced an alien encounter—and *Lexie* was the alien.

"Business," Zoe said, silencing them. She fixed her thick-lashed, overly made-up eyes on Lexie once more and said, "We have to switch the club date to Wednesdays at three o'clock. Thursday is my spa day. I'm sure you can understand that."

Then she turned on her three-inch heels and swung her hips all the way back to her side of the line, groupies in tow.

Wilson shrugged. "Hey, treasurer's cool."

"It's bogus," Lexie said. "We don't even need one. We don't *do* anything." He nodded, then shuffled into the crush of students rushing to class. What did he know, anyway? All he cared about was stepping into liquid. Maybe all surfers were extraterrestrials, too. How else could they manage to balance on a skinny, wet board pushed by thousands of gallons of tidal force?

Before he turned a corner, Wilson waved and Lexie was reminded of his earlier kindness. He wasn't so bad. After all, maybe *she* was the alien. How else could she appear so smooth when she felt as if a volcano were bursting in her chest?

A succession of different Lexies pop up in jack-in-the-boxes, controlled by an unseen hand. Pop: A confused Lexie cries. Pop: A laid-back Lexie Web-surfs. Pop: A freaked Lexie wonders who is the laid-back Lexie. Pop: An introspective Lexie watches all the other Lexies.

But which one was the real Lexie? And who was programming her, anyway?

5

LIFE IN THE BUBBLE had been annoying before, but Lexie had never imagined how bad it could get. Once word of her misfortune got around school, she was no longer invisible. Now her peers' Monitor B's reeked of sympathy, and their pitiful stares followed her wherever she went. Instead of being just a freak, she was now the motherless freak. Nevertheless, she forced herself to attend the first Virtual Club meeting. It was the least she could do to please her mother.

As she made her way toward the computer lab, Lexie couldn't help thinking about what a raw deal her mom had gotten in the daughter department. Lexie knew her mom had secretly hoped that her "real" daughter—the one lurking inside this grungy computer-nerd-of-a-kid—would someday emerge like a delicate butterfly shedding its ugly cocoon. This "real" daughter that her mother was meant to have would have been, of course, a clone of her. That is, if Lexie hadn't suppressed the daughter that liked pink oxford shirts and blue pleated skirts, gardening, and almost any social event, from dances given by the country club's youth group to the school prom. Hey, she might have even been the next homecoming queen! Lexie understood what her mother had wanted; she even felt sorry for her, in a way. If Lexie had done all that work—having a baby and raising it, feeding it, changing its diapers and all—she wouldn't have wanted it to turn into her.

At times, she had tried to do things her mother's way. Once she had agreed to learn needlepoint, which her mother often did at night "to relax." Her mother had taught her an easy stitch, and Lexie had gotten caught up in the blissful image of the two of them sitting together by a fire, chatting about life, as their needles went up and down, in and out. But as she sat there staring at the white net with the wide holes and the pink cat face printed on it, she had to fight the urge to scream. What was the point? To make a little pillow to place on the little chair in her little room in her little house in this little neighborhood on this crazy prison planet? It was too absurd.

By the middle of the second lesson, she had yawned and with feigned nonchalance put the needlework down on her chair. "I'm tired. I think I'll go to bed," she had said. Then she had tiptoed out of the room, as if she didn't want her mother to notice that she was leaving, and never tried again. Her mother had never mentioned it, either. Just sitting together, however, in any room that contained one of her mother's prized needlepoint pillows, Lexie sensed deep disappointment on her mother's Monitor B.

But what could Lexie do? She couldn't rewire herself—and even if she could, deep down she didn't want to. Someone had to worm through the all-pervasive *Bubble* program, and it might as well be her.

As she stepped into the computer lab, the inviting sound of keyboards clicking stopped altogether. Two dozen pairs of eyes were trained on her, and although nothing was said, Lexie scanned the club members' collective Monitor B output and knew that they felt sorry for her. Dual-focusing on a point of nothing, she hurried toward the front row and slumped into an empty seat. The tap-tap-tapping of her fellow club members resumed at once.

Lexie booted up one of the school's computers and was surprised to notice, mixed in with the relaxing drone of cyber-hum in the room, a stream of disturbing real chat coming from the back.

"They're on sale!" a girlish voice said. "So? Use your credit card. Tell your mother black leather pants are an investment. That's what I did. . . ."

Lexie peered curiously around the consoles. To her amazement, she spotted Zoe sitting at the back of the room, her blue-jean-covered legs on the desk in front of her, chatting on her cell phone. She had actually showed up? Her 12-step Mall-aholics Anonymous meeting must have been canceled.

Zoe caught Lexie's eye and looked at her with such directness that Lexie felt like a mirror in which Zoe was examining herself. Embarrassed, Lexie quickly averted her gaze and entered her password.

"You've got mail!" said the e-postman, a message that—spam or no spam—never failed to give Lexie some degree of pleasure. Of course, sometimes it turned out to be useless dreck. Today, she realized, as she scanned down a short list of messages with sympathetic titles from several club members, was one of those times. Without reading any, she deleted them all.

An odd clacking sound caught her attention, and with sudden horror, she realized that Zoe's metallic platform sandals were slapping against the linoleum floor as she sauntered in Lexie's direction. Without a second to spare, Lexie rolled out her antiinvader force field to repel the unwanted interference.

It was a technique that she observed all earthlings using, although most people weren't aware of it. In fact, she had learned it from her mother. Once in a local grocery store, she had watched her mother recognize someone, then slam out an invisible wall, freeze-framing the field around herself. Somehow her mother's acquaintance got the message, because even in that small store the two women never crossed paths.

Concentrating hard now, Lexie sent out a strong repellent vibe, but Zoe kept coming. Lexie pushed out her heavy-duty tractor beams, practically shoving them right up Zoe's nose, yet she was truly impressed when Zoe plopped down right on top of her desk.

"I'm way glad to see you!" Zoe said, crossing her long legs and flicking her shiny hair over her shoulder.

"What are *you* doing here?" Lexie said.

"Can you believe my mother switched my spa day without telling me?" She swung her leg back and forth in a sweeping rhythm, as if it were a metronome in whose groove the entire club was supposed to rock. "The faculty rep keeps checking up, so I've been stuck here and I really have to get my legs waxed." This was said in that privileged tone that assumed you would never dream of objecting to her wish. Then, as if trying to convey her sincerity, she slowed the beat of her leg. "So you can, like, *be* the president."

Lexie restrained the impulse to push her off the desk. "I don't care anymore."

Zoe shrugged her lithe shoulders. "Whatever." She stilled her leg and pulled a CD-ROM out of a red silk Chinese bag. "Here," she said, handing it to Lexie. "I thought you could use this, you know, to remember your mom. . . ." She floundered, and Lexie was caught off guard by the genuine sympathy on Zoe's Monitor B.

Lexie turned the plastic box over in her hands and read the title: *The Virtual Personality Program.* On the cover was a smiling figure draped in a silly hooded cloak decorated with cartoonish stars and moons. He was waving a magic wand that spread golden light, illuminating once-drab photographs of grown-ups and grandparent types, as well as a few of children at play.

"Thanks," Lexie said. "It seems kind of weird."

"Yeah, it's for when you miss somebody," Zoe said matter-of-factly. "You just, like, make a virtual personality of them, sort of like a copy, I guess, and feel better."

"You make it sound so easy."

"My last Step gave it to me, but I don't do computers. He actually thought I might miss him. Sweet guy—he sort of treated me like I was his daughter." She paused to roll her eyes. "But, you know, whenever my mom gets rid of one, I have to get rid of him, too. All their stuff goes out! Except this. I liked the picture of the purple coat." She took a deep breath and resumed swinging her leg.

But why would the Diva give her something? Then it clicked: It was a bribe! Zoe wanted help maintaining her image. Disgusted by such gross, manipulative behavior, Lexie was about to toss it back when she noticed a familiar look on Zoe's pretty, painted face: *loneliness*. Were they running the same program? No way. Zoe was the School Queen and Lexie was nobody. Lexie wanted to ignore her but found herself drawn in as Zoe continued.

"We're on Step number three now, you know. I can't get into any sentimental stuff. Grown-ups are way too unpredictable. Trust me, you've got to keep one step ahead of them. Don't get too attached; then it's easy."

As if she had accomplished her Nerd Mission, she slid off the desk and, without another word, left the classroom.

Lexie stuffed the disk into her backpack. "Whatever."

All of a sudden, she needed to retreat to Ajna-Mac's haven. She headed out and began walking the few miles home. As she treaded the sidewalk, past house after house, each with its two-car garage and its landscaped lawn and its hidden occupants, she experienced her usual suffocation from the still sameness. Did aliens live in cookie-cutter molds like earthlings? She doubted it. They probably lived in large pods where everyone contributed according to their programmed talent. Each pod would have numerous cooks, housekeepers, gardeners, accountants, doctors, and so on, all of whom served the group. The efficiency of their imagined ways filled Lexie with longing. Instead of tearing down thousands of trees to build dozens of wasteful homes, aliens would build one large complex with miles of gardens to serve one big pod family, and no one was ever lonely there. She passed a particularly dead-looking, traditional-style family home. As she focused on its coordinating paint trim and its geometric shrubbery, Lexie feared that one day she, too, would inhabit such a sterile environment.

Fast-forward: I open the door of that very house, and a young girl who resembles me, my daughter, runs past. "I love you, Shiny Diamond," I call out. She mumbles something and jumps onto the waiting school bus.

A man, my husband, dashes past me and drives off in his Mercedes. I stand there waving good-bye for a long time—maybe forever—until I realize there's no one there. I pick up my briefcase and lock the door. As I walk down the driveway toward my Volvo sedan, I begin to disappear. Bit by bit, starting with my feet, I vanish. The car door seems to open by itself, and the driverless vehicle slowly heads down the street.

L EXIE BALANCED THE cheap chopsticks with practiced
ease between her fingers and navigated a piece of lemon
chicken from its white plastic-coated box toward her
mouth. Midair, a drop of yellow, sugary sauce plopped down on
top of her Game Boy.

"Ugh!" she said. She dropped the chicken, the chopsticks
clattering after it onto the table, and wiped her e-toy clean.

Her father's eyes arched over the top of his newspaper and
then sank once more behind the impenetrable sheet of tiny sym-
bols and numbers that always exerted an uncanny power over
his mood. If the numbers, which represented money, went up,
he was "bullish," and then he and Lexie might actually share a
few words, maybe even a smile. A "bearish" report, however,
meant that they would each stay locked away in their respective

worlds as they had for the last six months since Lexie's mother had been gone. Not that Lexie minded the quiet; she had nothing to talk about with her dad anyway. How could she relate to someone whose frequency was ruled by the up-and-down swing of arbitrary values assigned by a piece of paper?

She was sure their Alien Rulers had devised this strategy, a sort of sleight of hand so that humans would never notice the awesome power of their own Internal Source: It was like throwing a dog an old bone; the dog could bite you, or even attack you if it chose. Instead it was happy chasing after a dried-up, marrowless bone. If humans ever realized the stupidity of spending their lives amassing piles and piles of money to buy more and more useless junk to fill bigger and bigger, ugly, wasteful houses, Lexie was sure they could break the stranglehold of their Bubble Masters. But how could people like her father ever understand, when they buried themselves in little cubicles from nine to five (the best part of the day, for God's sake!), trading percentages in companies that manufactured pointless objects? For what? To buy a better Mercedes? What was wrong with the last car, which was thrown onto some heap of rusting metal, polluting the earth? She guessed that aliens not only conserved their resources more wisely than humans but also utilized Energy Chips which, unlike money, actually increased their well-being.

She studied what little she could see of her father; the frown lines on his forehead told her he was in a bearish mood. For a moment, she considered educating him in the finer points of Bubble Economics, when he muttered, "Wal-Mart is down a point and a third."

Why bother? Better to leave him on his side of the table and keep to her own. In fact, if she ignored the junk food that had rooted out her mother's healthy snacks in the kitchen canisters, and forgot that her mother prohibited video games during meal-time, she could almost convince herself that she and her dad were simply having another dinner alone, just as they had done many times before when her mother had worked late.

"How's school?" her father asked, his voice filtering through the news pulp.

Lexie didn't respond; she just didn't feel like pretending to talk. She stabbed another piece of chicken with a fork, then together with *Vega, The Warrior Goddess,* nuked an incoming enemy star trooper. Her father appeared to have forgotten her once more as he rattled the pages.

A few minutes later he said, "Is there anything you need—clothes, books, food?"

Not again. Once a week he asked this question, and each time it pounded into Lexie's brain like stones being dropped from a cliff into a shallow pool. When would he understand it was Mom's business to help her with those things, not his?

"No!" she said.

"Oh." Her father paused and seemed to search for the next item on his mental checklist called "Dealing with Lexie." More newspaper rattling—perhaps it activated his brain—and then he said, "Don't you have to do your homework now?"

"Nope." Since when did he care about her homework? Lexie concentrated on the battle raging on the small video screen, trying to squelch the one inside of her.

"But you have homework every night, don't you?"

Overwhelmed by the parental reconfigurations she was forced to make, Lexie drifted into an unconscious Sleep Mode in which she only had enough energy to play her video game. If her father spoke to her, she was oblivious. But minutes later, when his paper landed on top of her Game Boy, she could no longer ignore him.

"Lexie! I'm talking to you!"

"What?" She threw her hands into the air in defiance. She knew her father would be relentless until he got an answer; that's what he said made him successful. So she stuffed her mouth with vegetable chow mein and laid it out for him.

"Yes, I have homework, like, almost every day," she said. "No, I don't have to do it tonight. I already did it during study period. If I need help, I'll ask you, okay?"

"Okay," her father said. His B-read was so vacant that it roused Lexie's suspicions. Sure enough, to her disgust, his voice downshifted into Adult Speak, as if she were too dumb to understand him in Real Talk.

"Honey," he said. "I want to address the issue of compatibility." Lexie groaned. The last thing she needed was for him to bug her about her social life, too. "I know your mother and you had been working on this, but I want to approach it from a different angle. I want to try and expand our little circle and allow others, close friends we're *compatible* with, to come into our lives. By practicing compatibility at home, you'll find it easier at school. What do you think?"

Lexie looked at him as if he had been invaded by hostile Intergalactics and said, "I don't have any friends."

"Exactly. But I do."

"Whatever."

"One special friend in particular. Someone I met a few months ago."

Before he could explain, he was distracted by the sound of a car driving up their driveway. "In fact, I invited her over," he said with a nervous glance toward the front door. "I think you two will be very compatible."

The doorbell rang, and he rushed out of the kitchen.

Good, go away! thought Lexie as she vaporized herself back into virtual warfare. She was flying low over a deserted range when her audio detected an unusual shift in her father's voice, which floated in from the foyer. She peered around the corner and saw a pretty woman with curly red hair standing by the front door. From her tight blue jeans and clingy ribbed sweater, Lexie guessed that she was younger than her mom, or at least she didn't look like she'd had any kids.

Lexie didn't know which was more disturbing—the way this

woman flashed her brown eyes at her father, or the golden glow that emanated from him. He stood deathly still, in a daze, and Lexie figured he was being blinded by the extraordinary whiteness of the woman's teeth, which she bared like an animal on the prowl. Lexie had surfed enough miles to know a phony when she saw one, in any dimension! She watched, bewildered, as her father hurried to usher the stranger into *her* house and close the door as if he were afraid she might get away.

At the sight of Lexie, they stopped. "Oh, this is Lexie," her father said, startled, as if he had just remembered her existence. "Lexie, this is my friend Jane Lewis."

"Hi," said the woman, holding out her hand to shake. "So you're Lexie. I'm so happy to meet you at last. Your dad is always bragging about you."

"He is?" Lexie said.

Jane smiled. "You bet."

Dad bragging about her? She didn't think so. He barely knew she existed. The woman was lying. With the clarity of mind sharpened during a whole childhood of surfing, she labeled Jane as a factor with which she could never compute, merge, or interface. She blinked at Jane's slim, freckled hand and pointedly stuffed her own hands down the back pockets of her jeans.

Seemingly undaunted, Jane handed Lexie's father a round plastic box. "I baked you a pecan pie," she said. "I hope you like it. It's my specialty."

"You baked it?" he said. You would have thought she'd won the Nobel Peace Prize.

"Oh, I love to cook," she said. "Especially for people I care about."

Lexie rolled her eyes. How could her dad be compatible with this horrible female intruder? This Jane was a totally unacceptable option, and Lexie would simply have to delete her as soon as possible. She must have time-warped, however, because she realized that Jane was already sitting in the kitchen, in Lexie's mother's very own chair!

"No!" she cried as Jane thrust a knife into the pie. "My dad has high cholesterol! Mom said he could have only low-fat."

Jane stopped and looked at Lexie's father, her big eyes questioning him. Lexie's once-sensible father scoffed at the sound advice.

"Let's not be fanatical," he told Lexie. "It's been years since I've had a real, old-fashioned dessert. Once in a while, it's okay." He turned into a gummy bear as he looked at Jane. "Besides, it's not every day a beautiful woman comes to your door bearing homemade sweets."

"Thank God!" Lexie muttered to herself. She stood apart from them, watching in disgust as her father hammocked his adoring face in his palms and pushed his elbows across the table toward Jane, practically falling in the pie. He giggled with her as she toyed with the size of his slice, moving the knife wider and wider until she finally cut a jumbo piece. *Gross!* thought Lexie.

Jane's voice dropped to a confidential whisper. "I don't think you'll find this to be an ordinary pecan pie. No common Karo syrup was used here. I only use a special maple syrup, Sleepy Hollow."

There was a quiet pause in which Lexie was comforted by the feeling that both she and her father were looking at Jane like a foreign organism. Whoever heard of Karo syrup?

But Lexie's father quickly dashed any illusion of them being in sync. "Really?" he said, full of admiration.

With a pang, Lexie realized that, as usual, there was a huge wall between them. Whereas she had decided to Drag the weird bug to the Trash, her dad had decided to Save it.

Jane presented a dark, amber bottle as if it were a trophy; on its label a mischievous sprite, wearing a maple-leaf dress, collected sap from a tree. "Oh, you've never had real maple syrup till you've tried Sleepy Hollow maple syrup," she said.

What was wrong with her father?

Jane, wearing a maple-leaf bikini and a saccharine smile, tiptoes on high heels down a beauty contestants' runway. She pauses in front of the judges to show off her prized syrup. "Pick me," she says. "Not only can I seduce any man I choose with my homemade, Sleepy-Hollow-maple-syrup-infested pecan pie, but I'll also entangle him in my sticky web so that he'll never be free." As she heads back up the runway, I trip her and she falls flat on her face—scoring a lousy six.

Lexie watched the gooey substance ooze out of the bottle as Jane soaked her father's slice with it. Her father took a big bite, syrup dripping from the sides of his mouth, and made embarrassing noises like a total fool.

"Ummm, aaah, wooo, yummy! A real heart-attack pie."

"That's not funny, Dad!" But it was way obvious that her brain-dead father had developed an immunity to her objections.

"Sleepy Hollow?" he said. "All this sugar, I'll never sleep again. Talk about misleading advertising."

Talk about misleading your brain with your sexware. First of all, it was really shocking to even *think* about her dad being interested in women. Lexie didn't think that he *wasn't* attracted to them, but she didn't think he was, you know, a *guy*. She certainly had never seen him act like one before. Yet here he was, acting just like any other dumb lover boy in her school. This was more than Lexie could handle. It was just too weird.

Jane held out a piece of her poison to Lexie. "Maybe you'd like to try it?"

"Duh?" Lexie said.

Lexie's father telegraphed his displeasure with that backpedaling smile he used whenever she did something socially incorrect in public. The accompanying text had long ago been hardwired into Lexie's brain. It simply read *Behave*.

"C'mon, one piece won't hurt you," he said, urging her with a sudden up-twist of his lips, which meant she might be rewarded later if she behaved now.

"But it's bad for us," she said.

Why didn't the rules apply anymore? If her mother had been there, she would have trashed the pie. No doubt about it. So why did this woman's presence delete the standards that her mother *and* her father had always insisted Lexie follow? If Jane had offered her some drugs, would her father have shoved that in her face, too? Here, kid, get high; the nice lady brought us some "far-out" drugs. The illogic of the Parental Dating Game totally messed with her brain.

Zoe was right. Grown-ups are way too unpredictable. There was nothing to do but eject from their world, which was, like, garbage in, garbage out, and retreat to hers instead, which was, like, logic in, logic out.

"I've got a ton of homework to do," she said, ignoring her father's surprised look.

Jane jumped to her feet, once more offered her hand and, as if giving a school cheer, said, "I'm really glad I got to meet you. I hope we can be friends!" Then she, too, used Adult Speak: "I'm so sorry about your mother, Lexie."

Caught off guard by this lavish display of attention, Lexie was surprised to find her hand clasped in Jane's. She jerked it away, as if her body were rejecting a rotten organ transplant.

Why leave, anyway? Lexie told herself. After all, it was her house. She stood her ground. "Well, good-bye, Jane," she said.

Any idiot would have understood that the party was over. But not Jane, who seemed immune to any B-output. Instead she offered that obnoxious, blinding smile. Perhaps she was a new Pet Prototype.

Lexie glared at her as if they were two cars playing chicken on a single-lane road, their eyes like headlights gunning each other. There was only room for one of them; someone would have to abort her mission—or both be crushed.

"It's, uh, kind of late," Lexie said, bearing down, pedal to the metal. A tense moment passed. It seemed neither would budge.

At last, Jane declared her defeat. "Well, I guess I'd better be going."

"No, please stay," Lexie's father said, virtually pushing Lexie off the road. "I insist you have a piece of pie with me."

"Okay, great idea," Jane said, with a giggle.

Yeah, he's, like, Einstein, Lexie thought as she stormed out of the kitchen.

L IKE A VIRULENT VIRUS, Jane's presence mushroomed in their lives in the following weeks. With the cleverest of strategies, she made herself more and more useful around their house until there was only one free zone left: Lexie's bedroom, and Lexie spent even more time than usual there, seeking refuge. One warm spring night, she felt dangerously close to maximum exposure to Jane's alien energy, and if it hadn't been for webrider's calming presence, she would have had a major meltdown for sure. She e-mailed:

> i think they went into the living room. i can hear
> them laughing. omg, my dad just turned on some
> disco music. i'm going to puke.

Then, for the hundredth time, she ran to her bedroom window, hoping Miss Maple Syrup had left. But Jane's bright red convertible Jeep still stuck out in the driveway below like a bad case of zits. Cursing her fate, Lexie turned away to find a quick response from webrider.

> maybe your dad and Jane are just friends. i mean,
> who would play disco on a date?

Wishing it weren't so, she typed:

> only my dad.

True, he was no Romeo. Still, there had been definite romantic bleeps on the redhead's Monitor B.

> later, diamondstar.

Her friend signed off, leaving her all alone—with them.

Help. Lexie pleaded with Ajna-Mac. *Get rid of Jane before her sticky vibe contaminates my force field.* Then who knew how many Negballs—those yucky, negative balls of polluted, grown-up gunk flying around the atmosphere—she might attract. Negballs, which were mainly composed of fear, always, always, always caused some kind of mental and spiritual contraction. They sounded like this: *What makes you think you can do it?* or *You're no good.* Pure poison.

In fact, Lexie's last memorable Negball attack had severely reduced her fearless rollerblading. Her mother, watching her one day as she cruised along the beach path, had called out to be careful; people often fell and broke their wrists. At once, Lexie had feared her computer typing would be hampered if she hurt herself. As the Negballs bombarded her, she had visualized herself on her Inner Screen, falling from a spin and breaking her arm. And true to the power of Negballs, within a few minutes she had suffered a bad fall. Up to then, she had never fallen! She hadn't broken anything that day, but she didn't enjoy her blades as much after that, either.

Over time, using her acute powers of observation, Lexie had taught herself to counterbalance any Negballs that were lobbed in her direction with powerful Posballs. Posballs were clean, positive thoughts like: *Good things will happen to me,* or *If I try hard, I can do it,* or *I'm going to help people, not hurt them.* In order to remain free of the insidious and relentless identity-conforming programs in the Bubble, it was essential to create your own steady stream of Posballs, especially after suffering a Negball attack. Posball vs. Negball—a pretty cool balancing trick.

Jane was like one gigantic black hole of Negballs, and though Lexie fought hard to resist the gravitational force by focusing on loving thoughts of her mother, she was already weary from the struggle. Even now, as Lexie's father's booming laugh, mixed with Jane's gleeful giggle, floated up to Lexie's open window, she closed her eyes and strained to picture her mother's smiling face. Better still, she plucked the photo from her bulletin board of her mother in Maui and stared at it. Then it struck her: What was it Zoe had said? *It was for when you missed somebody.* With a glimmer of foolish hope, she searched for the CD-ROM that the Diva had dumped on her. Maybe she could—how did Zoe put it?—make a "copy" of her mom to help ward off Jane's Negballs.

She found the childish-looking case with the picture of the silly sorcerer on top of her chess set. As she loaded the disk into Ajna-Mac's hard drive, he gave his characteristic e-laugh. A double-click and she was in. Swirling stars trailed by cosmic dust shot across the screen as a cheap Muzak rendition of "As Time Goes By" played over the title. The program's host appeared in his magician's finery. His e-voice was scratchy and sort of scary, too, like some cheap sci-fi video.

"Welcome to The Virtual Personality Program," he said. "Let us weave your memories into an eternal presence." Lexie rolled her eyes as he continued with a flourish of his wand. "Whom do you wish to immortalize?"

"Whatever." She typed her response: Mom.

"Please click on Visual and upload a photo of your beloved."

From her digital file she uploaded the photo of her mother on the beach in Maui and, with wistful longing, watched as her smiling image filled the screen. Another double-click, and she highlighted her mother's face with a bright, golden light.

"Excellent! Please connect the source, select Record, and play an audio segment of your loved one."

Once more she played the DVD of their summer trip. She clicked on the Record button and heard her mother say, "You're worth every pound, every wrinkle, and every worry." Lexie let the DVD run for a few more minutes until she guessed there were enough of her mother's sound bytes recorded for the alchemical procedure to work.

"Please tell me what you want to hear Mom say."

She whispered the words as she typed: I love you, Shiny Diamond.

She paused, remembering the countless times she had heard her mother say those cherished words. She could recall the feel of those words as they pressed into her, holding her tight. They had a smell—like the lingering night-blooming jasmine that trailed around her bedroom window—and a taste—like hot chocolate. They weren't just words, they were the actual walls of the virtual home in Lexie's heart. She would have given anything to have heard her mother say them once more.

"Please wait while I perform my magic."

As she waited for her virtual mom to appear, a long, random list of times Lexie had waited for her actual mom to do something scrolled down her Inner Screen: to drive Lexie somewhere; to tuck Lexie in at night and read her a book; to explain some pop historical reference, like Woodstock; to give her some money. . . . The list was endless, and Lexie noted the high percentage of her young life in which she had been entirely dependent on her mother. It was as if they had operated in tandem, as a single mechanism: Lexie wanted something, her mother provided it. Now Lexie wondered how her own gears would operate without the key Missing Piece.

"Lexie! Alexa Aurora Diamond, answer me!" her mother said, a familiar edge in her tone. Those exact decibels had resonated in that exact sequence with that exact emphasis ever since the days when Lexie was a toddler and had stubbornly hidden behind the curtains. Without a doubt, it was Mom!

And with all the nonchalance and belief in the wonderful-world-of-anything's-possible-if-it's-programmable that her daily diet of gigabytes had instilled in her, Lexie answered her. "Hi, Mom."

At the same time, she lost sight of her mother, who merged into a drifting news photo of the president giving a speech. Her mother shouted over his voice, "Honey, how are you?"

But the fragile connection was damaged. *This is crazy*, Lexie's Conformed Self told her. This was her logical voice, the one that navigated the so-called real world around her. In fact, the whole Bubble was designed to eliminate your Real Self and force you to operate with a Conformed Self, just like everyone else. And although Lexie's Real Self willed her to believe in her mom's presence, her Conformed Self knew it was impossible to see her mom online.

As her consciousness began to shift between the two Selves, her Personal Cursor jammed. Negballs, which her Conformed Self had empowered by filing them into her database at unguarded, self-doubting moments in her life, locked up her system: *You're not special! You imagined it! Your mother is dead!* Their cunning familiarity seduced Lexie away from The Light, which was reaching out to enfold her. The negativity crushed her. She was just a kid. She knew from experience to protect herself with some self-affirming Posballs, but that program was frozen. Paralyzed between two worlds, both Lexie's Real Self and her Conformed Self freaked as her Central Processing Unit began to crash.

"Oh my God!" Lexie sprang back from her computer. Was she having a close encounter? She fumbled with the disk drive, ejecting *The Virtual Personality* program.

"This is insane."

Lexie tried to stay calm, but she was overwhelmed. She was being towed to the edge of an e-abyss and would need a major power upgrade from a high source before she could leap across this chasm of faith. As if banishing both e-gods and e-devils, she shut down her computer, jerking her hand away from the cybercelestial fire raging within.

Lexie stood still, her mind spinning. In the quiet room, regret overcame her. As if she were moving her fingers across her mother's face, she traced the spot where her mother had been.

Mom, was that you?

She strained to recall the voice that had sounded so real, so safe. But it was already fading. Desperate to deepen that groove in her consciousness, she hit her Internal Replay button, pounding it over and over again. *Don't lose it! Save it!* she told herself. Her mother's disappearance had already proved that cherished sounds could be erased without warning. Concentrating hard, she tried to create a permanent audio file using the fresh memory of her mother's voice. But no matter how hard she tried, she knew it would never satisfy her.

What happened to us? Lexie asked her enigmatic e-Buddha. From within her own Self, a subtle answer was offered: *To travel this road, you must be fearless. If you continue, however, you will find the power within to understand.*

Perhaps a self-portrait taken years ago on a delayed timer—she couldn't say when—came into focus. For the first time, thoughts of her mother did not curl back upon her with a flame of sadness, singeing her. Her mother's possible appearance had illuminated an alternative path that Lexie had never imagined. Perhaps a whole new world of options existed on her Inner Menu. Maybe Oma was right: *Love never dies.* The formidable nexus of thoughts multiplying in her mind, like atomic fusion, left her dizzy.

Get a grip! she told herself. She flew out of her room, down the stairs to the refueling station.

L EXIE'S HANDS TREMBLED as she scrounged around in the fridge, studying the same-old boring foods over and over. She focused on a bunch of celery that seemed to invite her attention. Maybe the mind-boggling, celestial cybervision of her mom had been caused by a chemical imbalance; her mother always said it was necessary for humans to ingest green-colored things, and Lexie had had an almost greenless diet ever since she had left.

Scrolling through her inner file on MOM'S BELIEFS, she also recalled her saying that light-burn from overexposure to computer and video screens could lead to depression. Did depressed, malnourished people see supposedly dead people online? Just in case, she compromised on some celery to nourish her body and some chocolate pudding to make her happy.

But as she reached for them, something strong clamped down on her shoulder, and she screamed.

Her father grabbed her. "Honey, are you okay?"

"Jeez, Dad! You scared me."

He took a step backward with the unmistakable B-move that one took when confronted by a crazy person. "I just wanted to talk to you," he said. He cleared his throat in that unsettling, this-is-more-serious-than-you-know sound, and Lexie's sensors went on alert.

As she watched him filtering his thoughts, choosing the most kid-appropriate way to deliver his message, she wondered if he could handle hearing about this bizarre portal—or whatever it was she had discovered—to her mom. She projected his various responses. At the very least, he would insist that she was suffering from burnout and restrict her computer access. *Not a good idea*, she decided. No way could she afford to lose touch with Ajna-Mac, the only stable power source in her life—especially with Jane's Negballs darting around.

"What do you think of Jane?" he said, startling her.

"Duh? I just met her." She ripped off the lid of the pudding container and threw the question back at him. "What do *you* think of her?"

"I like her a lot," he said. "We're very compatible. I hope we're going to see a lot more of Jane."

While her father droned on about how wonderful Jane was and what a good person she was, Lexie alternated between munching on a celery stick and inhaling the brown muck, until she thought she would throw up. She hadn't realized how totally mental he'd gone. Maybe if she could communicate directly with his backup disks, she could doctor them; she just hoped they weren't too damaged.

"Don't you miss Mom?" she said, in plain text.

"Of course I do," he said. "But life isn't a fairy tale, honey. We have to go on."

Go on? Without Mom? Maybe it was worth the risk to tell him. "Well, do you . . . um, like . . . ever hear Mom talking to you?" she said.

Her father looked at her with that quizzical look that never failed to activate her defenseware—he thought he knew exactly what she would say and had already formed a judgment about it before listening to her side of the story.

"I mean. . . ." She struggled to find the right words to describe her amazing experience, but Bubble-language failed her. "Like it sounds just like Mom, and you know in your heart it just has to be her?"

"Are you feeling all right, Lexie?"

"Dad! Listen to me—I'm telling the truth. I sort of heard Mom talking to me."

"Uh-huh. . . ," he said, coaxing her to reveal more.

She paused and drew in her breath. Her father was staring at her through that long, distant parental telescope, and she felt like a millipede crawling on a lonely stretch of frozen intergalactic highway. She had to get through to him.

"I saw Mom online," she said, then added, "at least, I think so."

Her father's response sounded convincing, even helpful, but Lexie knew what he was really thinking.

Dad, Monitor A: "You know, honey, we've all been under a lot of stress, and it's obviously going to make us react in unusual ways. That's why we need to reach out."

Dad's Shadow, Monitor B: *My daughter is troubled; she needs help. Jane will be good for her.*

His deduction was insane; his system had already defaulted. But just because her dad's vision had become clogged with Bubble residue didn't mean she was going to let his doubts Windex her recent encounter with the Unknown.

"You know, it's possible," she said. "I mean, there are all kinds of unexplained, scientific phenomena. Physicists don't even know whether our universe is contracting or expanding. It might even be shaped like a donut and go round and round. So, like, why couldn't I hear Mom? Maybe she tried to talk to you, too, and you just weren't listening!"

Her father waited until she was finished, then spoke in a calm but commanding voice. "As a matter of fact, I have heard your mother lately."

He was still operational! Of course, he would have had the same fantastic revelations. After all, Lexie had been half-copied from her father's hard drive.

But as soon as he began with Adult Speak, she knew he had

only been teasing her. "Your mother told me, 'I'm okay. You and Lexie need to get on with your lives.' At least, that's what I *imagine* she said." He paused, letting that dreaded word sink in, before he continued. "If we could talk to your mom, believe me, she would understand that we need to allow new people into our lives, people who can help us. Please tell me you'll work on accepting Jane."

With a sigh, Lexie shut down her B-perceptors. What good did it do anyway to perceive her father's subtext when it caused her so much pain?

As so many times in the past when she had restricted access to a large part of her intuition, an ever-increasing hole was torn in her confidence. Her doubts festered there, multiplying like a destructive viral attack until, more and more, she questioned her instincts. And finally, trapped in a dank cave of confusion, she would lose her way at a dead end called "imagination." That was where her parents banished all her wild statements. When she was six or seven, she hadn't cared too much that *they* were wrong. But as she got bigger she had begun to fear that there was something wrong with *her*. Maybe it was her fault that so-called reality and her impressions of life's underbelly seldom matched. Unsure, she had learned to keep her mouth shut. And in this case, her experience had been laced with enough fear, and then overshadowed by her father's authoritarian conviction, that she betrayed herself once more and succumbed to self-doubt: *What an idiot I am. Of course Mom is dead.*

"Whatever," Lexie said, and raced back to her room.

HER FATHER'S FAULTY assumption that a mutant creature like Jane could help his "stressed-out daughter" was
demonstrated to Lexie several days later. She was walking toward the afternoon school bus when, to her horror, Jane
popped up on her radar. Red hair flying out of the open top of
her Jeep, she descended upon the school like a tornado and
screeched to a halt at the end of the car pool lane. Lexie
slammed out her force field, trying to block Jane from view. No
such luck.

"Hey, Lexie! Lexie Diamond, wait!" Jane said, waving her
arm like a wild octopus. Determined, she hit her horn several
times until everyone was staring first at her, then at her target,
Lexie.

With frantic speed, Lexie's Internal Analyzer processed the

available data and concluded that her dad was trying to interface his girlfriend with his daughter. Then it spit out her options: If she could just make it to the bus, maybe she could escape Jane's long tentacles. If she ran, however, Jane would suspect she was avoiding her and might make a scene with Lexie's father.

Jane maneuvered her car around the long line of vehicles and drove ahead along the school lawn, setting off a furious roundelay of honking. Just then, Zoe stepped in front of Lexie, shielding her from the unbearable onslaught of attention. Lexie wondered whether Zoe, who was embarrass-immune, was trying to siphon off the attention for herself. But at that moment, she smiled with gratitude at Zoe, who in Sisterly Mode shepherded her onto the bus.

Jane wedged her Jeep up alongside and called out, "Hey, Lexie! Come with me! Your dad asked me to pick you up!"

Lexie crouched as low as possible in her seat, trembling. Again Zoe came to her rescue. She leaned out of the window and lied like a pro.

"Lexie's coming over to my house," she told Jane.

Jane might be lame but at least she knew better than to dispute a diva's statement. "Oh, okay. See you later!" she said as she gunned her engine and drove off.

Before Lexie had time to recover, Zoe slid into the seat next to her, further astonishing not only Lexie, but the rest of the bus as well. Several of Zoe's groupies actually pointed at them. And

Lexie was sure that she saw a look of disapproval on Wilson's Monitor B. But Zoe, who was used to doing whatever she pleased, seemed oblivious to the effect she had caused.

"Your dad is, like, major WWGC," she said. "Widower With Girl Child; it's the fastest track to remarriage. Sort of like a divorce effect to the max."

Lexie blinked at her benefactress. *WWwhat?*

Zoe breezed through her analysis of grown-up dating patterns, which was based upon years of observation. "It's weird, but WWBC, Widower With Boy Child, is the slowest track; although they do remarry. Just like DMWBC, Divorced Male With Boy Child, they stay single a long time, too. But when you combine a single male parent with a girl child, the dad freaks. He doesn't know how to do the girl thing. He thinks you, like, need a new mother to look out for you, buy your lingerie and girl stuff." With a knowing look in her eye she summed up the situation: "Trust me: Your dad will be remarried in less than a year." The next closest thing to sympathy softened her jaded face as she added, "Don't worry—if you really hate his new wife, you can go to a boarding school."

Lexie choked. *A boarding school?*

All my stuff: **Star Trek** *chess set, collections of vintage Iggy dolls and magnets—everything is cruelly cut away from its spot and packed in boxes marked* LEXIE. *The boxes are stacked in the garage, where they gather mildew and spiderwebs until one day they're "accidentally"* *thrown out during spring cleaning. Roomless and stuffless, I forget who I am and have to wear a name tag. Twice a year, I visit my old home, staying in the guest room, but my Memory Chips are permanently downgraded.*

Lexie sank into such a sullen mood that Zoe soon wandered down the aisle, seeking more animated parts. Lexie observed the ease with which she crossed back over the line that separated them and once more assumed the role of Queen Bee.

Who knew a diva could be so helpful? So WWGC was the problem. If only Lexie had been a boy, maybe then she and her father would get along. He had probably wanted a son all along. Okay, next lifetime, she would be a guy. But wait—on second thought, she couldn't stand all that hair on her face! She immediately roped in that gender-switching idea before it got sucked up into the detailed file that she called NEXT LIFETIME.

It was a secret game she played by virtually adding desirable features, like a well-designed puzzle, to the Perfect Person she would be next lifetime. She wasn't exactly sure when she might download her awesome New Self, since she wasn't sure whether some kind of Recycling Option even existed. But if it did, she wanted to be ready. For example, at the top of her customized list was a hot body. It was obvious that whoever had been in charge of assembling her current components had been way lax in that department. Her fantasies were just an exercise in alternative reality, but she found them comforting. Maybe if her parents had kept a file called THE PERFECT KID they would have been happier with the result.

The afternoon sun flashed through the trees, creating a kaleidoscope of colored lights across Lexie's face. She squinted her eyes, aching to lose herself in the mesmerizing green, blue, white, and yellow mosaic fractals. If only she could ease the gnawing fear that Zoe's predictions had unleashed. Drifting into that peaceful part of her mind that had never changed since as long as she could remember—it was so blissful there—she resolved to convince her father that she was self-sufficient and didn't need another mother.

The bus rolled to a stop at the end of her street, and Lexie dragged herself down the aisle toward the exit. She looked at Zoe, hoping for some sign—of what she wasn't sure—some recognition perhaps that they had shared a real moment. But Zoe only seemed to look right through her. *Invisible again*, Lexie realized. Maybe she could only be seen when other people wanted to see her. Maybe she didn't even exist.

Wilson buzzed past her, nearly knocking her into the driver. Happy to be reminded she was real, after all, she followed him off the bus. She watched as he ran to his house, grabbed his skateboard from the porch, tossed his backpack, and took off down the sidewalk on his wheels. It must be nice to be so simple, she thought, staring after him. He probably still did paper and pen. Yeah, she decided, he was like a big kid. Perhaps he felt her energy directed at him, because he turned and smiled at her with such warmth that Lexie wondered if she had ever seen any-one smile before. Too stunned to respond, she simply watched him sail away.

With renewed confidence—a real smile from someone can do that—Lexie stepped into her kitchen and threw out the pile of take-out menus that had become the primary source of food for her and her father. Cooking, however, was not basic to her programming. This was another way in which she failed to live up to Bubble Standards. For sure, no one outside the Bubble cooked; aliens only had to inhale energy from their rich, unpol-luted atmosphere. Eating was just one more clever distraction to keep the pets from noticing their captivity—breakfast, snack, lunch, snack, dinner, dessert. Who could plan a revolt when you had to eat so often just to stay alive?

Whenever Lexie had tried to prepare the simplest thing, for example, scrambled eggs, she would forget to factor in the pre-historic pace of Real Time. Waiting forever and ever for the eggs to cook, her attention span—which was cyberally infinite but actually deficient—would drift into hyperspace, only to dis-cover that the eggs were ruined. But now the thought of having that genetic malfunction, Jane, tapped into her life on a perma-nent basis made her anxious to get cozy with the Cuisinart.

First she rushed upstairs to her desk and performed her Access Ritual. As Ajna-Mac booted up and the familiar thrill of connection coursed through her body, she laughed to find her-self wondering whether she might find her mom online once more. Nevertheless, she replayed the images of her mother's appearance on her Inner Screen, analyzing them like a physicist trained to detect the slightest alteration in subatomic particle behavior. Having been forced from an early age to defend her perceptions from her parents' accusations, she was adept at spotting the subtle energy differences between real and pretend, and she could often settle the problem to her own satisfaction with laserlike swiftness. She was surprised now to feel so confused; she was resisting the truth. In her heart, Lexie realized, she *wanted* to believe she had seen her mom. Of course, emotional disturbances always interfered with a correct analysis.

Maybe for once, she admitted, her father had been right. On the heels of her self-doubt, a flurry of Negballs bombarded her until her head sank low and she collapsed in the swivel chair. *Dredge up some Posballs!* From the best part of herself a few trickled in: *I may not be beautiful but I'm smart. I see things most people don't. Yeah*, her Conformed Self taunted her, *see, as in imagine*. It was no use. She was fighting a brutal tide of self-criticism, and she had not yet learned to keep her head above water.

At least she had the consolation of a message from webrider. Despite Ajna-Mac's mailbox being full with the ever-present spam urging her to refinance her house or buy a guaranteed antibalding lotion, instinct told her she would scroll through to find her e-friend's message. It was just a feeling she had, like when people knew it was going to rain on a perfectly sunny day.

Even offline, she could sense whenever she had received a message from her. For the first time, however, she wished that her e-pal were walking through the door instead of sitting on the other end of some coaxial cable. Lexie could never want for a better online connection, but finally, she wanted a friend who could see all of her.

Webrider's e-mail made her laugh, anyway:

> my brother is obsessed with this girl at school. he's
> driving me crazy. he talks about her all the time. she
> barely knows he exists. so pathetic. what r u doing?

Lexie understood, as any cyberloving girl would, how absurd it was to spend all your precious energy thinking about someone you hardly knew. I mean, how could you like someone you had never even talked to? Where was the connection?

She summed up her response:

> your bro's mentalware is deficient. guess what? i'm
> learning to cook.

Still glowing from the effect of Wilson's smile, however, she added:

> could you ever like a surfer dude? a cute one?

She hit Send and went to work. She downloaded some Easy Peasy recipes, then began the most crucial part of her plan. Scooting around the Web, she gathered irrefutable facts, graphs, and statistics from leading online marriage therapists that proved, beyond a shadow of a doubt, how moronic it would be for her father to marry Jane. She was so grateful for all the data, and it was so neat, that she decided she would soon establish a website for other WWGC kids.

Lexie had long known that her mission as an elite surfer was to put as much truth onto the Web as possible. Truth was the cyberglue that held the whole Web together, not all the cables and modems and subscriptions—only the simple power of truth. And the more truth that was generated, the less fake the world would be, because whatever happened online was later reflected on earth: *as above, so below.*

If only her parents had truly understood the real purpose of the Internet. She had hoped that her mother, being such a compassionate person, would have gotten it. But whenever Lexie had had the urge to raise her parents' awareness beyond their petty little lives and explain so many references—which she had already seen them dismiss—in order to arrive at just a basic understanding of the truth, she felt utterly exhausted. She would sigh and think, *Why bother? They'll never understand anyway.* Now she had no choice but to enlighten her father, or else be doomed to a life of quantum fakeness.

Midway through her research, webrider finally responded with the question on Lexie's mind:

do you like this surfer dude?

Lexie rolled her eyes and replied:

he's clueless.

But then a picture of Wilson smiling at her flashed on her Internal Screen. She was surprised she had saved the image, but she had to admit it made her happy. She confessed:

> i like his smile.

Nevertheless, she agreed with webrider's response:

> keyword for surfers: brain-dead. hey, can you bake
> chocolate chip cookies—my fave?

Why not? She'd send her some cookies—their first physical contact.

> i'll send you my first batch! i need your snail mail.

There was no immediate reply, and Lexie assumed webrider was busy in her perfect life with happy parents and a dumb but real brother. At least webrider's parents seemed to be living happily ever after. Even stranger, Lexie had the impression that webrider got along with them. And while Lexie was genuinely happy for her friend, she was sad to realize that webrider would never completely understand her, no matter how much else they had in common.

A S LEXIE WIPED THE sweat from her forehead, she left
a streak of flour. Jeez, it was hot in this kitchen. Hot and
boring. She poured a thick puddle of pancake batter
onto a steaming hot griddle and watched it morph into a dark
saucer. She scooped it up with a flat-headed, long-handled
instrument and, feeling like a real chef, flipped it onto a plate. It
landed with a thud. She wiped her gooey hands on her mom's
favorite, worn apron and counted an even dozen. Pleased with
her achievement, she placed the plate of "Perfect Pancakes" on
the kitchen table next to a bowl of "Feel Good Fruit Salad" just
as her father strode in.

"Breakfast is ready!" she said, waving her arm across the
table with an extravagant flourish.

Her father laughed. "What are you doing up so early on a

Saturday morning?"

"I've got everything under control, Dad. Just relax." She held out a chair for him. "Sit down, please."

He shot her a quizzical look but managed a weak smile as she placed a short stack of cakes in front of him and poured a cup of thick, dirt-black coffee. Imitating Jane's pouring technique and sugary smile, she smothered the stack of blackened pancakes with Sleepy Hollow maple syrup. Everything was going according to plan. This was the day that she would debug the deadly virus that had taken over her life and reprogram her father's WWGC ways.

His anxious look soon melted into the satisfied, glazed-over one that humans wore when they stuffed their bodies with food, even when it was barely edible.

"Hey, what do you know?" he said. Lexie was too proud to catch any of his B-meaning.

"The sequence is all worked out; you just follow the steps." She grinned and tried a few bites herself. *Not bad.* But she was on a mission: Enlighten Dad. Eating would only dull her focus.

"If you're interested," her father said between mouthfuls, "I'm sure Jane would be willing to teach you a few things about cooking. She's a bona fide chef."

Lexie nodded in her noncommittal way and glanced at the stack of downloaded information piled on the counter to reassure herself. It would all be over soon; her dad would be insane not to dump Jane after the severe Reality Adjustment Lexie was about to give him. But as her father continued singing praises about Jane this and Jane that, Lexie, like a doctor standing by with a cure, could no longer bear to watch him suffer from his delusion.

She grabbed the precious antidote and, adopting the professional tone which she had often heard her mother use, said, "Dad, before you make any, you know, serious decisions about Jane, there's something really important you need to know. Just take a look at this."

She placed in front of him a chart—which she had discovered in some far-flung hole in the Web—and jabbed her finger at a series of dark bars. "It's clear what's happening to you. When a relationship ends, you get this, like, Polarity Effect, a positive/negative thing. You're wired to attract the opposite pole of your last partner. Jane is Mom's opposite—*that's* why you're attracted to her! You can't help it! You're just experiencing a Polar Opposite Reflex Shift. But don't worry, all you have to do is let your electrical currents cool off until you can make a better selection." She finished with a satisfied smile.

Her father was smiling, too! He got it. But then he started chuckling, and Lexie's delight wavered as she detected the negative vibe on his Monitor B.

"Lexie," he said, shaking his head. "You can't dissect something as special as my relationship with Jane. Authentic feelings can't be confined to a graph. You just don't understand about grown-up things."

"We don't need Jane around anyway," Lexie said. "I can totally take care of myself, I swear."

"We do need her. I need companionship and you need a friend."

"A friend? I'll get friends. I'll rent a friend. I'll start a Friend Website!"

"Believe me. It will be wonderful having Jane in our lives."

Just then, Jane's voice rang out from the foyer with a cheery trill. "Hello!"

"What's she doing here?" Lexie groaned, loud enough to make sure Jane would hear. "I thought we were spending the day together."

She was silenced, however, by her father's angriest telegraph: his eyebrows spiked upward, warning her not to make a scene. An old childish impulse to zing him back with "I wish you were dead!" erupted but fizzled at once. She had permanently deleted that feature when her mother left.

The minute Jane stepped into the kitchen, her father cut his anger and pasted on an adoring smile. The mute sweethearts stood smiling mindlessly at each other, as if they had donated their brains to science. When, Lexie wondered, would the mischievous alien boy—who was obviously playing this nightmarish joke on her—log off her life?

An earth-obsessed teenage alien lounges on his star bed aimlessly flipping a remote Web Viewer among billions of pet earthling channels. For no good reason whatsoever, he hits Continuous Play when my Personal Screen comes into view. Bored and mean, he dumps a continuous stream of Negballs onto my channel. He even sets up Universal Links so his derelict buddies can also torture me. Let's play "Get Lexie!"

Something shiny pulled Lexie's attention back to Jane. She was dangling in front of Lexie a pretty knit cap with miniature round mirrors embroidered on it.

"I was hoping you'd help me," Jane said. "A few months ago my boss sent me to India to shop for our catalog, and I found these great hats. I think they'll be a big hit with kids, but I'd like to see one on you. Would you try it on for me? If you like, you can keep it. Please?" Her request was made in the same seductive voice Lexie had heard her use on her father.

Okay, the hat was really cool. For sure, if Jane hadn't been attached to the other end, Lexie would have snatched it up in a flash. Still, she hesitated, held back by the instinctive knowledge that if she accepted the gift she would automatically transfer power to Jane.

The more you got from someone, the more that person owned you—not like a slave; it was way subtler than that. It was a simple matter of energy flows, and Lexie was a young priestess in the Religion of Energy. She knew that every relationship, from the cosmic to the mundane, had a balance sheet. Once you accepted something, a gift, a favor, time, *anything* from someone, they scored the credit, not you. At the moment, her account with Jane was zero-zero, and that was how she wanted it to stay. The last thing she needed was to swing the balance in this clever cyborg's favor.

Jane held the cap up to Lexie's face and brushed the soft wool against her cheek. Lexie's skin tingled, as if a spell had been cast.

"Look, the blue matches your eyes," Jane said.

Lexie's lust blocked her better judgment, until only one thing bounced off the hat's enticing mirrors: her Shortsighted Self had to have it. How many debits would a dumb little cap add up to, anyway? Couldn't she just do some nice, meaningless, nonstressful thing for Jane in return, in order to cancel out this silly, tiny, unimportant gift?

The Temptress wagged the alluring bundle in front of Lexie's nose, teasing her. Lexie reached out, but her hand hung in the air, hesitating. For God's sake, it was just a stupid hat. She grabbed it and slid it onto her head, imagining how that woman in *The Scarlet Letter* felt pinning a red *A* onto her dress. The hat marked Lexie as a traitor, if only to herself. She hurried to a mirror in the dining room and stared into it, bedazzled—for the first time ever!—by her own reflection. She actually thought that she looked kind of cute.

You're selling out! Mom would be horrified, her Dutiful-Daughter-Self accused her. No, she was just being polite. *Relax*, she told herself; *it isn't like I've traded with the devil: my soul for a supermodel's body.*

Jane and Lexie's father peeked into the room. "You look adorable!" Jane said. Lexie didn't really care what Jane thought, but since Jane was a woman, her opinion gave definition to Lexie's fuzzy Self-Image Enhancement.

Jane studied her. "What do you think, Lexie? Do they have enough eye appeal to sell in a catalog? Would you order one?"

See? Now Lexie was expected to converse with her. She ripped off the hat. "I don't know. I never bought anything from a catalog," she said.

"Oh, no? But you like it, don't you?"

Why lie? Karma Kong had enough to deal with. "Yeah, it's cute," Lexie said, giving it back to Jane.

"No, no, you keep it. I really appreciate your help. I think they'll sell, and you'll be the first girl in your school to have one!"

Lexie's father beamed at her. "It looks great, Lex," he said. And Lexie was irked by his smug B-text: *See, good compatibility with Jane.* Then he squinted his eyes, with a gentle nod—a coded reminder that translated into: *Say thank you!*

Lexie mumbled a sufficient "Um, thanks," hating herself for having chucked her principles—and so easily—for an absurd body adornment.

"My pleasure!" Jane said, and it sounded so true. Hey, it was true. Jane's Monitor B confirmed it. But why, Lexie wondered, wasn't Jane wearing the victorious look of someone who had bagged a precious Energy Chip? Didn't she want to marry

Lexie's father, become her evil stepmother, and send her to boarding school? Perhaps Lexie had misjudged her. Maybe she needed to observe Jane with a more objective eye. After all, only the truth kept her free from total Bubble immersion.

"Have you been anywhere else really cool besides India?" Lexie asked.

"Honey, Jane's been around the world three times in the last five years," her father said proudly, as if this woman were his possession. "She's a true adventurer. No nine-to-five for this girl."

Jane waved her hand, as if she wanted to stop Lexie's father from bragging. Lexie had to admit it sounded like a cool life.

"I love to travel," Jane said. "Last year, I went to Australia and New Zealand. I bought some Maori handicrafts in Whakatane that sold really well."

"Hey!" Lexie's father said. "I've always wanted to go to Australia and dive on the Great Barrier Reef. Let's plan a trip!"

"All of us?" Lexie said, her voice rising into her soprano register.

"Why not? I've always wanted to go there. Jane can be our guide."

Oh, how Lexie regretted her weakness. Jane's Power Account had mushroomed with that clever hat trick, and now they were all vacationing together!

"Why don't we go for a bike ride?" her father said. At Lexie's furious stare, he added, "The three of us."

"Good idea," said Jane. They both looked at Lexie.

"Uh, my stomach hurts," she said. It wasn't true, but Lexie preferred to have big, bad Kong squat on her rather than to spend time with this slippery chameleon.

"Lexie, you were fine two minutes ago," her father said, still smiling.

She shrugged her shoulders. "Appendicitis? It's sudden."

"We're all going, now." He was clenching his teeth through his ever-present smile. Was it, like, glued on his face whenever Jane was around? At least, Lexie consoled herself, his Father Mode was still operational enough to have detected her lie.

"Please, just a minute, David," Jane said. She whispered in Lexie's ear. "Can I talk to you in private?"

What did they have to talk about? Curious, she let Jane pull her down the hall.

Jane spoke in a reassuring and confidential voice. "Are you having menstrual cramps?"

Lexie was caught off guard by the direct, personal nature of Jane's question. But then it occurred to her that maybe this was how women talked to each other. "Um, not right now," she said.

"Are your cramps usually bad, though?" Jane said with unrelenting interest.

"Sometimes," Lexie said.

Jane brightened. "Oh, I have the perfect remedy: homeopathic cell salts." She fished in her bag and pulled out a small, plastic bottle filled with tiny white pellets, which she handed to Lexie. "Works like a charm. I give it to all my girlfriends."

Girlfriends? Once again, Lexie was surprised by Jane's apparently authentic friendliness. Maybe Lexie was stuck unknowingly in some outmoded program. Maybe, like her father, she was also subject to some random Bubble effect— *Motherless Girl Hates Girlfriend, MGHG,* programming. Yes, the faulty logic of it suddenly struck her. Her dad liked Jane; he had liked her mom. Lexie liked her mom; maybe Lexie could like Jane. She didn't even know Jane, yet she had already made the decision to delete her! Now that, she scolded herself, was primitive Bubble Behavior.

"Okay, thanks," Lexie said.

"If you ever need any help, I'm here for you," Jane said.

Once again, she was befuddled to verify Jane's sincerity with a clean B-report. Why then couldn't she accept this woman? She thought of an essential maxim of the Elite Websurfer's Code: *Only an open mind can plug in.*

So why couldn't she?

S HE WAS WORRIED that the back gate to her house might squeak on its hinges when she opened it, announcing her presence. She peeked through the slats in the fence. As far as she could see, the coast was clear. Lexie just didn't want to be seen. Truth was, she didn't want to come home. She had stayed out late after school, riding her bike, playing video games at the pier, but now twilight was falling. She nudged the wooden door open and cringed as, indeed, it betrayed her with a telltale squeak. She paused for a moment—no one called out. Like a thief, she slipped into the backyard, but her efforts were in vain. There, in a corner of the yard, she saw Jane pruning the roses.

"Hi, Lexie!"

Ugh! With the force of her feelings, Lexie slammed the gate shut and strode across the yard without a word. If only she

mind. If only she could talk to her mom, she would know what to do. She whispered in her faithful friend's ear, "What if Mom really is out there? Help me find her, Ajna-Mac."

So they pooled their resources, and together Lexie and Ajna-Mac went gliding through every connection they had, asking here and there if anyone had seen or heard of a really rad celestial portal. But like global explorers seeking uncharted land, they found no route.

As they continued their search, an instant message popped up from webrider:

whassup?

Of course, it being a Friday night, Lexie was not surprised that they were both home online. She also knew she could confide in her best friend:

hey, this sounds a little wacko, but i might have once accessed a dimension beyond the web—a super pure realm of energy. no clue how to access it again. any ideas?

And Lexie's faith in webrider was proven, once again, by her response:

you got the power, diamondstar! i've heard rumors of an awesome window to the ultimate power source. someone had to be the first to hook up; maybe it's you. i'll troll around. possibility is everything.

Webrider's answer reminded Lexie why she found solace in their connection. There was no criticism, no indirect meaning, only acceptance. Why, she wondered for the millionth time, couldn't everyone in this cagelike existence just let everyone else be? Look at the humans' own pets: was a Labrador retriever better than a border collie? Each dog, like each human, had a unique, perfect design. From the infinitesimal vantage point of Lexie's little spot in the Universe, it was impossible to view the whole plan, but she was convinced the Alien Masters had designed Earth's Super Kennel with enough room for all types of humans.

Bolstered by webrider's encouragement, Lexie focused more clearly on her screen, as if a dull film of doubt had been wiped clean. A huge folder on her desktop, called LATER, went 3-D on her. She moused over and clicked it open. As she scrolled through it, however, nothing struck her as relevant to her problems, and she wondered why she had opened it. But a sudden jolt went through her when she noticed a link she had made at least a year earlier to a Wiccan site. *Oh yeah,* she recalled, *witches and spells and stuff.* And then, as the magic of her own ways took effect, she realized why the file had called to her—*a Banishing Ritual!* It promised to get rid of unwanted interference, or homework, or people . . . like Jane. *Wouldn't that be nice?*

Lexie had learned to save seemingly random particles that drifted her way, only to discover later that, in fact, they held some meaning in her life. It was as if, surfing through her universe, she would get in the groove and connect to certain things floating past her. Something—a name in a newspaper, a picture on a poster, an item in a store, an unusual website—would suddenly come alive and call attention to itself with a subtle tug at her awareness. If this clue had no relevance to any current situation, she would enter the data in her LATER file.

She didn't always catch a clue. Sometimes it went over the wave and she missed it. And when its intended purpose would later materialize in her life, she would regret not having listened to the earlier signals. *Oh yeah, that's what* that *was for,* she would understand, vowing to be more alert next time. For when her virtual senses were really acute—not her five ordinary hardware senses but the ones that she relied upon for her survival, the ones that allowed her access past the ordinary version of life— she managed to score stuff that she would later redeem big-time.

Of course, a clue didn't always work. But when it did, Lexie felt a great sense of satisfaction. It was as if some information had escaped from the future and drifted downstream to her in the present, preparing her for what was to come. She often wondered how this process worked, but it happened with such regularity that she just accepted it as one of the perks of being an Elite Surfer.

Landing at the Wiccan site, she was greeted by Merry Meet and Welcome! She clicked open the Banishing Ritual, and as she read it, a sly smile crept across her face. Perhaps she had never more fully appreciated the wonder and reliability of her Universal Server, which consistently sent her such amazing, accurate clues. She had definitely been "on" the day she caught this one.

She printed the magical directions and ran into her closet, hunting for a required doll. Lying forgotten at the bottom of a wicker basket, she found an old Raggedy Ann. It even had a red-haired resemblance to Jane! Next she needed a candle, which she had on her bookshelf, left over from an old science project. She lit it, placing it on top of her purple throw rug, and turned out the lights. As she closed the black bedroom curtains, she couldn't help feeling ridiculous, but she was desperate enough to try anything, no matter how bizarre.

Lastly: an item that Jane had touched. The knitted cap! Lexie plucked it from her backpack. She knew she should trash the dumb thing and rid herself of its nefarious karma, but she liked it; she even looked good in it. To compromise, she plucked off several of its small mirrored decorations and added them to the "brew."

Sitting cross-legged on the floor, she picked up the doll, and with the keen concentration she had developed to annihilate the enemy in video games, she projected a picture of Jane onto its one-button-eyed, sweet smiling face. Then she ripped a hole in its head. Full of determination, she stuffed the mirrored chips inside and quickly closed it with a safety pin she nabbed from the hem of her jeans, careful not to let any of Jane's energy leak out. Substituting a black shoelace from an old pair of Nikes for a black ribbon, she wound it around the doll's head until it looked like it had had surgery in some Third World war camp. If this worked she promised to volunteer for the Senior Citizens' Computer

Literacy Program every Saturday, all day for a whole year.

For accuracy's sake, she reread the bewitching directions; there was no room for mistakes. Then, in a low, quiet voice, she chanted: "With harm to none, my will be done. I hereby banish Jane Lewis from my life. Your words cannot harm me. Your thoughts cannot harm me. You cannot harm me." She clutched the doll's neck tightly, feeling both a little silly and a little powerful, and repeated the invocation. You never knew, it just might work.

The last part of the ritual required Lexie to prick her finger and drip blood onto a piece of paper. She ripped a piece of paper from a spiral notebook, but since her pain threshold was zero, she simply signed her name with a red pen. She also signed Ajna-Mac's name, since he had participated. As best she could, she folded the paper into a heart shape and held it over the candle until it caught on fire. Then she dropped it into a metal wastebasket.

Well, that was fun, she thought, wiping her hands clean. She hurried to her window to see if, by any chance, Jane was speeding away in terror. To her utter disappointment, Jane's Jeep still stood in the shadows below. Thinking perhaps there might be a delayed reaction (after all, it was Lexie's first try), she waited several minutes for Jane to appear. All of a sudden, the smoke detector on her ceiling rang with a loud high-pitched shriek. She turned, aghast to see the throw rug in flames, and realized she must have knocked over the candle.

"Help!" she screamed, and threw her arms around Ajna-Mac.

Her father burst into the room, with the Girlfriend right behind him. "Call 911!" he told Jane.

Instead, Jane picked up one end of the heavy hallway rug and, with a commanding force that startled Lexie, yelled out to Lexie's father, "Grab the other side." Lexie watched, trembling, as they dragged it on top of her burning throw rug, smothering the fire.

"Quick thinking!" her father said. Jane was smiling from one stupid ear to the other. "Boy, are you good to have around in an emergency. Quick mind, quick body. What a woman!" He gave Jane a hug. Turning to Lexie, he said, "For God's sake, what were you doing in here, young lady?"

Lexie's first thought was: *a magic ritual that will get rid of Jane,* but her father's enraged face inhibited her. "A science experiment," she said in a good-little-schoolgirl voice. She would take whatever punishment Sir Kong dished out, she bargained, if only her lie would not dilute whatever magic power she might have worked.

"Next time, do it at school!" her father said. He was pissed. "You could have burned the whole house down. And I doubt our insurance would cover a science experiment!" Scowling, he carried the charred remains out of her room.

Great, all her little experiment had done was win Jane a few more good karma credits. What did it matter? Lexie was just another lost pet. She had no control over her life anyway.

W HILE LEXIE SLUMPED into a funk in her room, which reeked from the smell of burned rug, Jane cleaned up. She dusted, made a laundry pile, and swept the wood floor. Out of the corner of her eye, Lexie watched her, half-resenting her and half-grateful for the help.

When the room was back in order, Jane perched on the edge of Lexie's desk. "Are you okay?" she said, with obvious fake caring.

Go away, Lexie telegraphed in Bold Text. But her glare seemed to bounce off Jane's rubber shield. Didn't she get it? Or had they stripped her of all sensitivity at the Alien Detention Center?

"Can I do anything for you?" Jane said.

Yeah, as a matter of fact, Lexie thought . . . and a hellacious command was rolling down her tongue when she heard Ajna-Mac play the syrupy rendition of "As Time Goes By." She rushed to her e-mate's side and watched, puzzled, as *The Virtual Personality* program's trademark appeared on her computer's screen.

Hello? She had *not* clicked it open! She would have liked to have a reason to yell at Jane, but she was sure she hadn't touched her computer, either. Oh no, maybe Jane's cybernetic body was messing up Ajna-Mac's signals. She had better get her skinny fish-stick hips off the desk ASAP.

"You have to leave *now*!" Lexie said.

Jane jumped up and took refuge at the door. "I'm sorry, Lexie," she said. Then she got all serious. "I really hope we can be friends."

Lexie glanced at her Monitor B, struggling to stay observant. But she was so distracted by Ajna-Mac's malfunctioning that she was incapable of computing Jane's output.

"What for?" she grumbled, and shut the door in Jane's face.

Lexie stared in amazement at Ajna-Mac, who was shining with the same luminous light that had tricked her before into thinking she'd seen her mom online. But that was a program default, virtual insanity, wasn't it? Whatever it was, she was mesmerized by it. The light intensified into a brilliant silvery glow, which seemed to pour through celestial cybergates, carrying with it a crystal of light that multiplied before her eyes into . . . *Mom?*

"How's my Shiny Diamond?" her mother said. Before Lexie could freak, or reply, or do anything, a bouquet of flowers advertising an online floral shop sped right at her mother. Just in time, she caught it.

"There's so much traffic out here," she said, tossing the bouquet, which was sucked up by the stream speeding past her.

Perplexed, Lexie stared at her mother, who, upon closer inspection, appeared to be standing in the middle of a rapid river of images. Her mother gave her a reassuring smile, and this time she understood, as any child would: *That was no image; it was Mom!*

In the throes of an epiphany, she cried out. "Wow! Mom, it's really you."

"Yes, it's me." She had to yell to be heard over the steady hum of cybertalk that threatened to drown her out.

"But how—?" Lexie said.

As she had so many times in the past, her mother seemed to read her mind and answered the question Lexie couldn't even form. "For a while I got lost in cyberspace," she said. "You know, access is really jammed, but I'm finally learning to navigate this crazy Web."

Lexie was freaking, beyond comprehension. Her mom was on—no, *in*—the Internet? She watched as her mother avoided colliding with the Statue of Liberty, which drifted past under a logo for "I♥NY."

"Wait a minute. This is . . . impossible!" Lexie said. Her natural instincts had been squashed for so long that her Higher Self had to struggle to plug in. A huge, clever Negball assailed her: *If you felt isolated up till now, with your virtual vision and unique view of the world, won't you just end up lonelier than ever if you dare to explore this new dimension of consciousness? Hit Quit and save yourself from rampant weirdness.*

"Honey, trust your instincts!" her mother said—as always, saying the right thing.

In that moment, Lexie couldn't have felt closer to her mother if she'd been sitting on her lap. They were connected—deeply, permanently, eternally connected. It would never be broken. *Love never dies!*

The e-powers had revealed to her the basic truth of life: Love was the true power source. She lifted her head to cyberheaven and laughed out loud. No longer would she feel doomed to be an accidental, antlike drop of ectoplasm hurled about in the cosmological pinball game. At long last, she saw The Light and it was rad. In that moment, Lexie was transformed from an extraordinary but trapped nerd into a freed Virtual Believer.

The joy of being found, however, was quickly replaced by the fear of being lost. What if her mother was pulled away once again by some unseen presence?

Tears rolled down Lexie's face. "I miss you so much, Mom."

"I miss you too, honey, more than you can imagine," her mother said, struggling to hold her space within the ever-moving circus of Web images.

Just then, there was a tap at her door. "Are you all right, Lexie?" Jane said.

Feeling frisky and full of herself, she called out. "Yeah, I'm just talking to my mom." There was no reply, which suited Lexie just fine.

"That was Dad's girlfriend, Jane," she told her mother.

"Oh."

"I hate her."

"Maybe you just need time."

"Dad has lost his mind. Oh my God, if he could see you, too."

"Lexie, I'm sorry to say this, but I doubt your dad will listen."

Sad but true, thought Lexie. In a flash, however, she saw a way to make him pay attention. "Mom, where is his college trunk?"

Her mother smiled, in that conspiratorial way they had often shared about his foibles. "Tell him I put it in the bottom of the canoe."

And then they both laughed—oh, it felt good. Her mother was back. In fact, she had never left. She was just transformed.

Just then, an advertisement featuring a beautiful girl driving a brand-new convertible popped up next to Lexie's mother. Before she could react, the car ran over her. Lexie gasped—her mother was gone!

She lurched toward the screen. "Wait! Mom! Come back!"

But she was nowhere to be seen. How would Lexie ever find

Cosmic Energy Source in some kind of awesome mind-share program. She simply had to follow the path of least resistance and let it do its thing. The Main Operator, with an omniscient view, knew when, where, and how to siphon off just enough available energy and send it in her direction. Therefore, despite the seeming paradox to having intention and persistence, surrender was the next major requirement.

Still, Lexie wanted to see her mom *right now*. She burned with curiosity to know what her mom had wanted to tell her. Yet all she could do was trust that there would be another online visit. Maybe it took practice, this surrendering stuff.

Then, remembering the awesome information her mother had given her, she flew into action. She ran downstairs and stopped short in the living room at the horrible sight of her father and Jane kissing on the couch in the family room. Yuck! Zoe was right: her dad was totally WWGC.

Her father and Jane jumped apart, as if Lexie had beamed a wall between them with the indignant look in her eye.

"Lexie, we were just, uh. . . ," her father said.

She plugged right in: "I saw Mom online, for real."

"What are you talking about?"

"I saw Mom online again, just like I told you. Only this time I have proof. She said your old trunk is in the bottom of the canoe."

"Honey," her father said, all but choking on his embarrassment, "you *remembered*. That's great."

Why? Why are grown-ups so slow sometimes? "I'm telling you the truth," she said. "Mom appeared on Ajna-Mac and—"

"Who?" Jane said.

Lexie rolled her eyes. "My computer's name is Ajna-Mac."

"Oh, I see," Jane said, totally not getting it.

"Look, Dad, why would I make it up? Like I care where your trunk is."

Her father looked hard at her, and she noticed his face suddenly soften as if he had just decided to let some poor abandoned cat into his home. "Okay, diamondstar," he said. "Why don't we go look?"

Puzzled by his sudden shift, she inspected his Monitor B: he felt sorry for her; he didn't believe the trunk would be there. But she believed, and her belief was big enough for both of them. The power of the entire Web had touched her, and she would just have to grace her father with it as well.

"Let's go," she said, leading the way to the garage.

But Jane held Lexie's father back and whispered something in his ear. Lexie didn't have to be psychic to know that Jane told him how crazy it was. She would have bet a month's allowance on it.

Her father patted Jane's arm. The B-read: *I know how to deal with this.* He nodded at Lexie, and they continued, but not before Lexie pierced Jane with a warning stare. *Don't mess with me.*

As she pushed open the garage door, her eyes drifted up to

the old aluminum canoe that was hooked to the rafters. This was absurd. Her chest tightened as her awareness mushroomed outward, accordianlike, into infinity.

The fate of my entire life is hanging in a canoe . . . Zap! . . . in this four-bedroom house . . . Zap! . . . on planet Earth . . . Zap! . . . in the solar system . . . Zap! . . . in the Milky Way galaxy . . . Zap! . . . in one universe . . . Zap! . . . dwarfed by innumerable universes. . . .

Chill! she told herself. But she was full of jitters as she watched her father place a tall ladder underneath the canoe and begin the climb. *What if the trunk isn't there? What if I only imagined it all?* Lexie's newly enlightened Self wobbled as old Negballs pelted her.

Level with the canoe, her father peered over the edge. A few agonizing seconds echoed in Lexie's loudly beating heart, and still her father said nothing. His lag time was unbearable.

"Dad! What?" she finally said.

He almost whispered. "It's here."

"Are you kidding?" Jane said.

"It's right here." He reached inside the canoe, and Lexie heard the old wooden trunk clank open. "And here's my trophy." With a confused look on his face, he held it high for them to see.

Why was her dad acting like such a zombie? Of course, she realized, he didn't understand that she was now a confirmed

Virtual Believer—no longer wired to the evolutionary programs that would lead her to a predictable future. Her poor father had forgotten what he must have known as a kid until he had lost sight of the Bubble.

She watched as he climbed down and handed the trophy to Jane.

"Jane, would you take this inside please?" he said.

B-translation: *Please leave so I can talk straight with the Kid.*

"Of course," Jane said, with a curious look at Lexie.

Sure enough, as soon as Jane left, he put his arm around Lexie and said, "Honey, isn't it possible that you saw the trunk being put up there?"

No way was Lexie letting even the tiniest Negball enter her force field ever again. Negativity, she was beginning to understand, was what kept her tethered to everyone else's "reality." She took a deep breath, telling herself that she was once more inhaling the sacred light of the Beyond. At once, she was rewarded with such a logical argument that she wondered if her mother could have sent it from Beyond.

"Dad, when was the last time you saw it?" A tenderness crept into her voice; he needed time to understand.

"Ten, maybe thirteen years ago," he said.

"Okay, I would have been a baby, or not even born when Mom put it up there."

Her father's brow wrinkled, as if he were considering the implications of Lexie's statement. After a minute, he said, "Well,

15

L EXIE SHUFFLED HER bare feet against the kitchen floor
and winced as her father pressed an ice pack against her
forehead.

"I'm fine, Dad," she said.

"A few more minutes," her father said. "We don't want you
getting a big head." He adopted a silly German accent. "Yah, dis
iz zee brain damage."

"Yeah, right!" Lexie giggled, and they tussled over the ice
pack.

For the first time in a long time, she had her old dad back.
He kissed the top of her head, and Lexie soaked up the warmth
of his love, filling up her nearly empty reserves.

There was a sudden switch, however, as he clicked once
more on distant dadware. "Tell me, Lex," he said. "How am I

137

going to leverage you and Jane together? You're both very important to me." Lexie's smile evaporated, yet he continued before she could answer. "Use this big brain of yours and be objective. Don't be so quick to judge her. Believe me, honey, I analyze situations for a living, and your old dad knows how to pick a winner." He grinned his winning grin.

"But you don't really know her," Lexie said, thinking of the terrifying impression she'd seen of Jane on the tennis court. "I mean, not *really*."

Her father sighed. "You can't understand; I never thought I could feel this way about anyone till I met Jane."

Never. . . ? She swallowed hard. "Not even about Mom?"

"It's different. Your mom is gone. I'd do anything to change that, if I could. But I'm finally happy again. Please, won't you try and accept Jane?"

"She's nothing like Mom."

"That's true. But if you would give her a chance, I bet you'd like her anyway."

What was Lexie supposed to do—pretend she liked Jane? So far, her acute observations of Jane had not yielded a clear analysis. Lexie's self-programming was too wobbly these days for her to trust herself.

Unfortunately, she had been corrupted by her well-meaning parents who, like most grown-ups, were trained to program kids by refusing affection to reality-dyslexic, code-breaking, Bubble-popping misfits. As Lexie had grown to feel more incompatible with the world around her, she had used her own *Personality* software less often, plugging into societyware instead. This gradual transformation was a built-in feature of the *Growing Up* program, and Lexie's current status was a predictable biware stage when kids often resort to a mixture of the two. Therefore, even when she felt quite sure of something, in the face of grown-up logic she often had to hack her way back into her own reality, past the no-that's-not-possibles and no-it-couldn't-bes.

She considered interrogating her father about the TENNIS INCIDENT when Jane walked into the room.

"How's the patient?" she asked.

"She'll live," Lexie's father said.

"Well, maybe some home-baked chocolate brownies will make it up to her."

"There's nothing to make up for, sweetheart."

"I bet Lexie doesn't feel that way."

Lexie hated it whenever grown-ups talked about her as if she were invisible. Now they were looking at her, waiting for her to say something. Why couldn't they just be direct? She might have answered them if they had communicated with her in the first place, but she knew the longer earthlings lived in the Bubble, the more their wiring became scrambled. It was as if they were gradually cut off from the Main Source until eventually they lacked the energy to confront people head-on, so they talked in circles instead. Kids never did that; they were in your face. And talking to a kid, whose wiring was less circuitous, often had the effect of accelerating a grown-up's roundabout way of delivering a message.

To make matters worse, the more direct Lexie was, the more she knew she would be punished. So she didn't say what she was thinking, either. Maybe that was how the whole sequence started: the kid talked out and was punished, then an insidious loop began until one day—indirect behavior.

"What?" Lexie said, staring back at them as she fought the urge to Direct Speak with, *If you want to say something just say it.*

As usual, Jane tried to laugh the tension away. "I just meant, you probably wish you'd never been hit in the head at all."

Duh?

The Alien Refugee Retrieval Force flies into our house. They stun Dad with an antimemory gun and grab Jane, who is making frantic, inhuman sounds. She shrinks to the size of a peanut as they carry her into their soda-can-size spaceship. The tiny vehicle vaporizes, and a small box, covered with blinking lights, hovers in front of me. It pops open and an e-voice says, "Sorry for the mix-up. We'll have your mom right back."

It was no use.

As Lexie shuffled off, her dad called out to her. "Are you okay, Lexie?"

She didn't bother to answer. There only one thing

that would make her feel better right now: Mom logging onto virtualbelievers.com.

She ran to see Ajna-Mac, but there was no sign of a visitation. She rewound the tape in the video recorder and made a note to buy a big supply of tapes the next day. For the rest of the day and night, she stayed in her room, glancing anxiously at Ajna-Mac. She refused to eat with her dad and Jane and survived on a hidden stash of peanut butter.

The next morning her father invited her to come with him and Jane to Sunday brunch, but Lexie risked Karma Kong's anger with a truly necessary lie about finishing a school project. The longer she sat vigil at her website, the more she felt compelled to stay by Ajna-Mac's side. Each random posting to her website made her heart leap, but there was no sign of her mom. Little by little, Lexie felt worn out. At last her e-guru emitted a loud beep and told her to take a break. She sighed with relief, shrugging on her backpack. *Keep up the good work, old friend.*

Within a few minutes she was riding her black and chrome mountain bike south along the path at Palisades Park. To one side lay the city, and to her right, below the cliffs and the ribbon of Pacific Coast Highway, was the Pacific Ocean, stretched out like an endless invitation. Riding along the edge of the continent never failed to give her hope: *I might escape from here.*

Approaching the Santa Monica Pier, she could hear the loud ratcheting of the roller coaster's metal gears as it pulled the cars upward, followed by the predictable shrill screams of its passengers. Soon she zoomed under the arch at the pier's entrance and felt the rickety bumps of the wooden beams beneath her.

The warm, sunny day had driven people down to the shore, and the pier was jammed with strollers; couples lazily walking hand in hand; families with kids carrying balloons and cotton candy; and buffed, tattooed guys in their tight T-shirts and gym shorts on their way to nearby Muscle Beach, parading for girls—or boys. As Lexie locked up her bike and walked to the pizza place, the familiar sounds and smells of her hangout began to ease the tension from her body.

"Extra toppings?" the girl behind the counter said. She had a metal stud on her nose, and when she spoke another one bobbed in the middle of her tongue.

"No," Lexie said, wondering if the girl's piercings marked her for a particular alien tribe.

She handed the girl her money and within a few minutes picked up her usual order of two extra-thick pepperoni calzones and a tall lemonade. Heading outside, she carried her food to a small red table, facing the amusement park to one side and the beach just ahead. She had sat at that very spot many times with her mom when she was a little kid. In those days, she couldn't wait to ditch her mother and run away to the Penny Arcade. As she gobbled down her food, she felt a pang of guilt. She would somehow make it up to her mom, if only she were given a second chance.

Entering the arcade, she was surprised to get a nod from Zoe, who was holding court among her fans. She averted her eyes as Zoe's crowd turned to see who the Queen had favored. As she shuffled away through the comforting din of the mechanical games with their promise of fair play in an unjust world, Lexie wondered if the Lip Movers were laughing at her. She pulled the mirrored cap that Jane had given her out of her backpack and hid under it, tugging it as low as possible.

At the pay counter, she handed a Hamilton to the old attendant, who was as familiar to her as the place itself. Hunched over, he rotated his arm like a joystick and gave her the pile of quarters with his knoblike hand. For sure this guy was going to end up as a video game next lifetime.

She nestled in the cubiclelike booth of *The Holy Grail* and inserted her money. She was a master at this game, and she smiled as her initials scrolled by, identifying her as the All-Time Top Player. Soon she was flying through virtual space. Escape. Lovely escape. Whooshing through tunnels, faster and faster, up ramparts, around corners, narrowly missing treacherous incoming enemy fire, she felt free. Just as she was about to scoot under a rapidly descending speared gate, loud, raunchy whistles from Zoe's group distracted her. *Crash!* She exploded against a virtual dead end.

Someone called out to her. "Hey, Lexie! Peep this!"

She glanced up and saw a meaty jock pointing toward the front arcade window. Lexie gasped. Outside, on display, her father and Jane were slobbering all over each other like a couple of dogs in heat. Oh my God, how embarrassing! Who kisses in front of the whole freaking world? They seemed completely oblivious to the commotion they were causing and the pain they were inflicting upon Lexie on her own turf. There was nowhere to hide, either. She could feel her face flush red. The obnoxious catcalls from Zoe's gang shook her to the bone with the deafening roar of a major earthquake. Everyone was looking at her!

Just then, Wilson and his crew breezed into the arcade, their board shorts dripping, wet hair slicked back. They quickly took in the scene. Lexie watched, dying, as Wilson looked from her to Zoe's gang to Lexie's dumb father and Jane.

"Check it out!" the jock yelled.

At that Wilson slammed into him, nearly knocking down the hefty footballer. A hush swept over the crowd as quick as an autumn fire fed by the powerful Santa Ana winds. The two groups sized each other up; it was an equal match. Lexie watched with neighborhood pride as Wilson once more slipped into his Peaceful Mode and signaled his guys onward. They pushed through the circle of angry meatheads.

He stopped as he passed near Lexie. "You all right?"

Speechless, she gave her ambiguous nod.

He pointed to his turf. "I'm over there if you need me." Then he strolled past.

At last Lexie's father and Jane ambled away toward the railing, overlooking the ocean below. The furious screaming in Lexie's head urged her to run—now!—and push them both into the watery depths. Instead she ducked back inside the video game's safe space.

She was conscious of internal explosions scorching her entire system. At the same time, she was fascinated by a parallel self-awareness of her exterior, which she knew appeared cool. Perhaps she had a built-in Diverter that kept her from going ballistic. Clever design. Wouldn't it feel better, though, if she just let it all loose and smashed herself to smithereens all over the arcade, the pier, Dad and Jane?

Suddenly Zoe strode over to her, probably to pick over her dying bones. She tried to delete the bouncing, blond supermodel-to-be, but of course that was useless. Divas couldn't be deleted. That's why they were divas.

"Never let your dad know how much you hate her," Zoe said, sounding as if she had memorized *The Teenager's Guide to Parental Battleware*. "Big mistake. From then on, you lose your advantage in any fight. Trust me, he'll always take her side because he'll assume that you're just trying to get rid of her."

Lexie looked up at her with a calm gaze that she suspected Zoe knew was fake and repeated the family myth. "Nah, my dad isn't like that," she said. "He's pretty fair. He's, you know, a stockbroker; he evaluates performance. If his girlfriend screws up, for sure he'll call her on it."

Zoe tossed a waxed forearm in the air. "My mother used to

listen to me until I tried to tell her what a jerk my current Step is. Unreal! She grounded me for a week. Now if I even, like, look at him cross-eyed, I'm screwed."

Once again, Lexie wondered why this shopping addict, who probably thought megabyte meant calorie overload, was dealing with her. Even if Life's Power Programmers had arranged this connection for Lexie's unknown benefit, she was determined to resist.

"My dad's girlfriend isn't so bad," she said.

Without missing a beat, Zoe said, "She doesn't give a shit about you."

"Um, well, I think she wants to be friends." Lexie felt totally lame.

Zoe narrowed her eyes. "Just remember, don't tell your dad what she's really like. He won't believe you in a million years."

"He totally will!" Lexie said, surprised to be defending her dad when a few minutes earlier the virtual desire to terminate him had raged within her.

Zoe simply shook out her long hair, as if she were ridding herself of their conversation, then sauntered back toward her clones.

Good riddance, Lexie thought.

But Zoe turned and called out. "Hey, cute hat. Fifteen dollars and ninety-nine cents at Target, right?" Then, as if she already knew the answer and had just been updating her shopware, she bopped away.

Lexie's ever-alert Internal Conflict Catcher clicked on. *Target?* Jane said she bought this thing in India to sell in a catalog. They didn't have Target stores in India, did they? Lexie ripped the hat off her head and flipped it inside out. A small bit of white fabric sewn into the seam caught her eye. The label had been cut out! Why would Jane tear out the label . . . unless she was lying about where it came from? But why would she lie about such a stupid thing? It was one of those illogical things that really bugged Lexie; it didn't compute. She stuffed the offensive, ugly cap into her backpack and logged the information into her expanding file on Jane.

A S THE SUN SANK OVER the Pacific, Lexie turned her
bike onto Georgina Avenue and groaned at the sight of
Jane's Jeep in the driveway. She just wasn't in the mood.
Even worse, Jane surprised her at the front door as if she'd been
lying in wait. *Creepy.*

"Can we talk, please?" she said.

Still smoldering from Jane's outrageous behavior at the pier,
Lexie pulled the knitted cap from her backpack and shook it in
an accusing way at her.

"My friend told me they sell these at Target," she said.

Jane sighed. "Yes, I know," she said. "The competition beat
us. As you might understand, I was very disappointed."

Lexie scanned Jane's Monitor B, but only got static. If Jane
was lying, she was very, very good at it.

more drained than Lexie's mother, bumped into her, edging her off the home page.

"Bob? Is Bob there?" the stranger said in a shrill voice.

Lexie watched, bewildered, as her mother said, with perfect cybermanners, "I'm afraid he's not here."

"Who are you?" the woman said, fixing her gloomy eyes on Lexie.

Lexie was too surprised to say anything. "She's my daughter," her mother said. "You'll have to excuse us; this is our site."

The interloper bristled with the air of someone used to having access wherever she wanted, virtual or not. Ignoring Lexie's mother's request, she turned her back to them, and Lexie's Web browser popped up on the screen. Lexie watched as it searched through Insurance Sales and then a list of hospitals. *Hello? Who is running Ajna-Mac now?*

"Who is that?" Lexie whispered to her mother.

"Another Lost Soul. We're all over the place," her mother said with a helpless shrug of her translucent shoulders.

This concept overloaded Lexie's circuits, and all she could do was enter the data in her LATER file. Of course, if her mother could be online, logic dictated that other people who had passed into the Beyond could be hanging out in cyberspace as well. Maybe these Lost Souls were responsible for somehow downloading the new software programs that, years ago, even the Internet Intelligentsia hadn't foreseen. Maybe they had even conspired to bring the Internet into being. *Wow*, Lexie realized,

I'm on the cutting edge of a major new techno-spiritual frontier.

At last the woman chose another site—with what commands Lexie couldn't tell—and vanished. Lexie's mother reoccupied her home page, as if she were adjusting a coat over her shoulders.

"I hope she located Bob," her mother said. "She won't rest until she finds him, or gives up. Making contact has been very frustrating up till now. You know, there's a story told here that one day a techno-babe will destroy the veil and connect our worlds. Who else could it be but my little computer wizard? I'm proud of you, sweetheart."

"Thanks, Mom," Lexie said in a small voice. And for once, their Monitor B thoughts matched: *If only it hadn't happened this way.*

Her mom's reddened face grew serious. "Lexie, I'm so sorry. This wasn't meant to be."

"What wasn't?"

"That's why I needed to contact you."

"I don't understand," Lexie said, with a growing sense of alarm.

"You already know what I'm going to say, don't you, sweetheart?"

"Yes," she admitted. With sudden and horrible certainty, she understood that her mother's absence had not been part of the blueprint for their lives.

"My new site wasn't ready," her mother said with a deep sigh. "It wasn't my time."

She nodded to a tall man in a purple cloak embroidered with glowing Chinese hexagrams who appeared to be in charge. He shook his head with the distraction of an absent-minded professor and punched some buttons on a large keyboard in front of the endless wall of screens. A bright light illuminated one of the millions of screens. With some advanced technology the highlighted screen grew more visible until Lexie had a clear view of it. A sign floated across it: #1001.XX-49Y, UNDER CONSTRUCTION. Then the screen went dark once more.

"The Webmaster showed you my screen," her mother said.

Lexie tried to absorb this information. But her mind felt sticky, like melting peanut butter, and with great effort, she extracted her response. "You mean . . . the car crash . . . someone hit you . . . on purpose?"

"I'm afraid so."

"What. . . ?" Lexie's shoulders shivered, as if an ice cube had been dropped down the back of her shirt.

"Are you okay, honey?"

Lexie nodded in her vague way. "But, Mom, who would. . . ?" She couldn't finish the thought; it was unthinkable.

"I don't have all the pieces yet," her mother said, "but I'm working on it."

"What about the woman who left the confession note?"

"I heard through the grapevine that she, too, was murdered. I'm hoping to track her down. I suspect that whoever killed her probably also smashed my car."

155

"Oh my God!" Lexie said. "I'll tell Dad! I'll show him; he'll have to believe."

Her mother simply shook her head. "Our connection exists through a very subtle vibration. You have to be listening with your heart. Your father is distracted right now. But there's one thing you can do to help, as long as you promise you'll drop it after that. I don't want you to be involved."

"What?" Lexie said. "I'll do anything. I promise."

Her mother paused and seemed to search her with such keen eyes—right through to Lexie's Monitor B. "Okay, but be careful," she said at last. "I want you to get a copy of my patient list to the police. Ask them to reopen the investigation."

"But, Mom, they won't listen to me." She was just a kid.

"Lexie, a few years ago I placed a letter for you in our safe-deposit box, in case of emergency. I never mentioned it to your father. Ask him to find it, and when he does, maybe then he'll help you."

"Okay."

"Don't be disappointed, though, if he still doesn't believe."

"He has to!"

"Just believe in yourself. You're always afraid people won't accept you, but you already have everything you need to find your way. Trust yourself."

In only a few words her mother had summed up the major glitch in Lexie's mindware. Only her mother could have done that. No one else knew her well enough.

"But what if I can't?" Lexie said.

At first her mother's face clouded over with that look she always wore whenever she was revising or downgrading the truth. In those moments, Lexie had always sensed the truth anyway. Once, years ago, when Lexie had rescued a baby bird from their lawn, she had come home from school to discover it was gone. Her mom had worn that same well-meaning but fake look when she had said, "It flew away." But Lexie knew it had died.

Now she prepared herself for her mother's cushioned response, but as she watched her mother's caution dissolve into a real response, Lexie recalled the number one element of the Elite Websurfer's Code: truth. Only truth fueled the highest access to the Web!

"Then you will just have to accept things the way they are," her mother said.

Never. Lexie was determined to avenge her mother's death.

"One more thing," her mom said. "Each patient has a code name, something that evoked personal happiness. It might be useful information to the police."

"Is the file encoded, too?"

"I'm afraid so."

"No problem; I can hack it."

Her mother gave her a wry smile. "There's no need. I chose something I would never forget, someone I will always love: diamondstar."

Suddenly her mother, who appeared to be increasingly

157

overheated and exhausted by the effort of their conversation, merged back into the screen until all that remained was her photo on the home page.

Lexie felt as if her circuits were being ripped out. She touched the screen, if only for a little comfort.

"I love you, too, Mom!"

But the only sound was her computer's quiet hum. She turned off her video camera and confided in Ajna-Mac, *There goes Mom, a virtual angel of the new e-millennium.*

Without a doubt Lexie had confirmation of how far ahead of the planetary learning curve she was. The Pet Masters were not about to let some lone surfer kid unplug The System that had been intact for billions of years just because she lucked out and found her mother online—especially if she was going to go around blabbing about it! All at once, she felt like a freak. She had been in the right place at the right time with the right equipment, and she had seen something that she wasn't supposed to have seen. She guessed that others, like Joan of Arc, had probably seen beyond the describable, too.

The difference was that Lexie's miracle had been online, and eventually, she figured, the e-elite would come around to investigate. Someday her supernatural program would be standardized and sold as an inexpensive CD-ROM. She pictured some cool packaging: Between heaven and earth, a colossal computer floats in the sky. A bolt of lightning streaks through it, illuminating the planet below. In techno-lettering the title reads: *The*

Virtual Believer's Software to the Beyond: Programming for Eternity. Then any user could be a free spirit! Just imagine how the world would change:

Logic rules. A planetary-wide ban on fakeness is in effect. Everyone operates on full capacity RAM. No one is punished for revealing true feelings anymore. Bragging on TV or in books about your malfunctions is forbidden. There are no strangers, only friends (we'll connect in this lifetime, or another). Nobody goes to sleep hungry or on a cold bench. All earthlings have a long-term, macro view of life and what's good for the planet. Fish can breathe in the clear seas. Amazing medical cures are discovered in the abundant rain forests. It's the end of oppression and war—only Posballs, everywhere. The truth keeps us Bubble-free.

At once she sent an e-mail to webrider with new details of her mom's website and visit. Inspired by her vision for a New World, she began:

revolt! spread the word, I've discovered a portal to
the motherboard!

SINCE HER MOTHER'S revelation the day before, Lexie had barely been able to concentrate on anything except her mother's words, which wound round and round in her head until she felt like a tight ball of string. *Not an accident?* She found it hard to believe that someone would want to hurt her mother. All during school on Monday she had been inventing possible explanations, but none seemed likely.

Back at home, she wasted no time in unpacking her mother's computer, which was stored in the garage. She lugged it up to her room and set it next to Ajna-Mac. Like siblings, she thought, charmed by their coziness. But her mother's computer stared back with an alarming dullness, like someone who had been ignored for too long. It was weird, she thought, how some people treated their dogs better than their computers. Dogs might be good companions, but only computers offered access to the one free channel in the entire Bubble.

In time she might rehabilitate the sad, lonely terminal, but for now, she booted it up with her usual Access Ritual. It was the least she could do. As she laid her fingers on top of the keyboard, she felt overwhelmed by her mother's presence.

A holographic image of Mom surrounds me, until I am like a small chip on her large grid. Her energy is flowing through me, helping me, leading me to the truth.

As Lexie opened her mother's PATIENT CODE file, a rush of energy surged through her—a clear sign of a big clue! The file was encoded, as her mother had said, but here, at last, Lexie stood at the crossroads between truth and imagination. She bubbled with excitement. If the password her mother had given her worked, it would confirm Lexie's hard-won belief in herself. With complete cyberfaith, she typed diamondstar. She held her breath as the computer's gears turned—and the file opened! Lexie laughed out loud. She was no more insane than this crazy upside-down world she lived in. In fact, she was the only sane person living among billions of pet robots!

On one side of the screen was an alphabetical list of code words, significant things that the patients identified with, like Tai Chi, Marzipan Pigs, Venetian Gondolas, and so on, and across from each one was the corresponding patient's name with a brief diagnosis. But there were dozens and dozens of names. Had one of her mother's patients been responsible for her death?

The temptation to probe deeper was too great. Yeah, yeah, she argued with Karma Kong, she knew she had promised her mom she would stay out of it, but didn't the means justify the end once in a while? She chose a few random names and searched the Web for data on them. But she didn't know what she was looking for or why. This job was too big to think small. Cosmic Backup would have to come to her aid.

She heard her father's car drive up to the house and, tingling with excitement, she printed the patient list, then bundled up her video equipment. She was glad she'd recorded her mom's visit—you had to think ahead if you didn't want to be domesticated by the Alien Masters. Once Dad saw Mom online, he would have no choice but to help Lexie—and then, one by one, other earthlings would wake up until eventually a revolt would spread, and perhaps they could be masters of their own fate. She couldn't help but marvel at the dullness that The Disconnected imposed on themselves. What a shame. So much potential, so little power.

As she ran downstairs to change the world, she found her father watching the news in the kitchen. As usual, the intoxicating smells of Jane's cooking filled the air. *Jeez,* Lexie wondered, *will Jane still like Dad once she's fattened him like a pig?*

"Dad," she began, "I have something very important to tell you." She handed him the hard copy of the patient code list.

162

"What's this?" he said.

She brimmed with confidence. All she had to do was let the evidence speak for itself. "Just read it, you'll see."

As he perused it, however, his face grew stern. "Lexie, where the heck did you get this?"

"Mom's computer. It was easy once she gave me the password."

"Oh boy," he said, loosening his tie. "You know that's impossible."

"How else did I get it?"

"You're the hacker, you tell me." He narrowed his eyes. "What was her password, anyway?"

Lexie puffed up with pride. "Diamondstar."

"Of course," her dad said.

This time, she called him on his subtext. "I did not guess it!"

"Anyone could have."

Grown-ups were so stubborn. She swallowed her injured pride and continued the fight for justice. "Dad"—here she paused and tried to imitate his sternness—"Mom said her death was *not* an accident."

Jane gasped, and Lexie caught her father giving Jane a sly nod. Even a grown-up could have read his B-output: *Poor Lexie, she imagines the craziest things.*

Ha! She would show him. "Mom's site wasn't ready—it was still under construction."

"Her site?" he said. "What are you talking about?"

"Never mind," she said with an impatient sigh. *Stick to a need-to-know basis,* she decided. "Look, we think one of her patients went bonkers."

Her father gave a nervous chuckle. "Honey, they're only as crazy as the rest of us."

"Well, maybe one of them was crazier than the rest; Mom wants the police to reopen the case."

Her father drilled her with a straight Monitor A look. "Lexie, I know it's hard to accept, but sometimes things just happen for no good reason. Life is a random series of meaningless events. If we had any control, we certainly wouldn't elect to have pain and strife. Life is like one of those video games you play—sometimes you win a game, sometimes you lose."

Lexie smirked. She never lost at *The Holy Grail* unless someone interfered. Her mom's personal game had still been in play, and someone must have interfered.

"No, Dad, the best players always win. Mom's time wasn't up. And I'll prove it to you." She hooked up her video camera to the TV.

"What's this, Lex?" her father said with growing annoyance.

"I recorded Mom's visit," she said, matter-of-factly.

She saw her dad and Jane exchange worried glances. Joint B-thought: *Lexie has lost it.* Never mind, she was ready to upgrade their systems with a dose of virtual belief.

She turned on the TV. "Just watch," she told them. "This will blow your mind."

The title of *The Virtual Personality* program floated across the screen accompanied by its signature song, "As Time Goes By." *That's strange,* thought Lexie, with a sinking feeling. She didn't remember recording this, or the e-Wizard who then appeared.

"Introducing Mom," he said.

At a flourish of his wand, the animated image of her mother popped onto the screen. "I love you, Shiny Diamond," her mother's avatar said in the disjointed voice.

"Very clever," her father said.

Jane added her cool appraisal. "That's nice."

"Wait, there's more," Lexie said.

But there was only an endless loop of the same image repeated over and over. Lexie uttered a low moan like a wounded animal. "No," she said, fiddling with the equipment. "It's been erased, I swear. I saw her! We spoke!"

"Lexie, it's all right—we understand," her father said.

"No, you don't!"

Her father and Jane waited patiently while Lexie employed her techno-skills on the inner workings of the camera and television. But nothing she did conjured up a recording of her mother's actual presence, and Lexie was reduced to tears.

"Honey, let's take a walk," her father said at last. This was such a radical departure—they *never* took walks together anymore—that Lexie agreed. Defeated and numb, she let him lead her down the sidewalk toward Palisades Park.

"It's easy to understand what happened," her father said. "If anyone could think like your mom, it's you. You deduced her password; it's that simple."

It was one of those rare instances when her father actually made sense. In fact, since her mom had left, Lexie had caught herself saying things a number of times that sounded just like her mother. At first it had only been a vague echo in her head, like the time she had scolded herself for leaving her dirty laundry lying on the floor. She had dismissed the impulse to compare herself with her mother because, after all, her room was a mess. Or the time she had felt impatient with her father for being late to dinner. And just that afternoon, when her hair had blocked the view of Ajna-Mac's screen, hadn't she found herself wondering, just as her mom had, how she could "see past that shaggy mop"?

When her mom had been around, Lexie had never copied Mom Speak, and it felt weird now, as if her mother had left behind a Memory Disk that had been inserted into Lexie's own mind without her knowledge or permission. Maybe that's what happened when someone you loved left: You automatically copied her database onto yours, so she could live inside you forever.

To her dismay, her Conformed Self agreed. *Yeah, Dad's right. You think like Mom. That's why you figured out the password.* But as Lexie's belief wavered, her Real Self reminded her of the last bit of data her mom had given her. *Try it!*

"Dad," she said, "Mom said she left a letter for me in the safe-deposit box at the bank."

"C'mon, Lexie," he said in a gentle voice. "Be reasonable."

"Can't you just look for it? It's my letter!"

He paused for a moment. "All right," he said with a sigh. "I'll look for the letter, but don't get your hopes up."

"Okay, but if Mom's letter exists, will you promise to do something? Will you contact the police? Mom told me to give them her client list."

"Sure, honey," he said, failing to disguise his B-content: *It won't come to that.*

Twilight crept across the western sky as they crossed Ocean Avenue into the park. Father and daughter treaded the sandy path among rows of royal palm trees, which stood in silhouette like tall sentries on the cliffs. Years ago they had walked here many times before as the city lights flickered on along the coast, forming a bright necklace around Santa Monica Bay. A cool ocean breeze swept in, and Lexie shivered. Her father put his arm around her and pulled her close.

"You know," he said, with yearning in his voice, "the day you were born was the happiest day of my life."

Lexie breathed in the salty air and watched the glowing pink rays dive over the horizon, chasing the sun. She smiled up at her father.

"You were a tiny thing, the most beautiful baby I'd ever seen," he said. "You never cried, not a bit. You just looked up at

me with those big blue eyes, as if you recognized me. Lexie"—
he paused and kissed the top of her head—"I've always loved
you. My leaving had nothing to do with you. Your mom and I
just grew apart; it wasn't anyone's fault. One thing we always
agreed on, though: We made a great kid."

Huddled beneath her dad's wing, Lexie felt happy. She hadn't
realized how badly she needed his warm hug. It penetrated right
through her and let her know that she wasn't invisible after all.
Because if somebody loved you, you really did exist.

And maybe she was crazy. Maybe her Old Life was obsolete
or enjoying the flip side of the coin somewhere else in the
world, while she was stuck with tails. And maybe this new life
was the Next Version. At least she could have her old dad back.

There was only one problem: Jane.

L EXIE SHIFTED WITH impatience in her seat and wished the school bus would move faster. Just hours from now, her fate would be revealed. Either her father would bring home her mother's letter, in which case he would be obliged to contact the police, or else he would be empty-handed, and then how would Lexie enlist his help? After suffering the humiliation of the missing video footage, she feared she would be at a dead end. And the constant nagging bothered her too. Since yesterday her Conformed Self had taken every opportunity to whisper in her ear: *If you didn't imagine Mom's visit, why didn't the video camera record it?*

She stared out the window as the bus passed one solid, looming house after the next. Their dense rigidity seemed to mock her heartfelt dream of spiritual cyberfreedom. The Bubble, she realized, had solidified over the centuries to the point where a lone rider had little chance of finding a pathway out. There was no denying that her initiation into the Virtual Believers Club had set her even further apart from the other human pets. But no matter how lonely she felt, she vowed never to defect to the Zombies' side. Even if she had to straddle her existence forever, with one foot in the cyberlight where she could clearly see—but was invisible—and the other in the harsh glare of well-adjusted life where she had to conform her vision—but was partially recognized—she must stay true to her beliefs. What she wouldn't give, however, to have just one other rider with extra-sensitive vision pass her and wave, like two hip phantoms giving each other a high five.

At last the bus stopped at her street. She jumped off—with only a superficial glance at Wilson—and ran to her house. She grabbed a can of soda from the fridge, drank it almost in one gulp, then wolfed down a large bag of cheese puffs. She microwaved some peanut butter, then some popcorn, mixed the two together, and ran upstairs.

She slid into her desk. *Hey, Ajna-Mac. Any news?* While munching her snack, she requested Access. *Beep, la, bee-beep, la, la . . .* the modem sang and the Iggy dolls danced. Lexie relaxed, happy to be back in her world. But there was no sign of her mother at virtualbelievers.com, only a message posted from webrider.

A bemused look crossed her face as she read it:

cool site, diamondstar! hey, cute picture. it's weird

to see what you look like after all these years.

Lexie didn't think of herself as cute. But she figured that she and webrider had mirrored each other for so long online that her friend, who must be cute herself, had mistakenly decided this was another thing they shared. Should they finally meet, for sure, webrider would be disappointed by Lexie's boring looks.

Lexie's buddy list showed that her e-pal was online, so Lexie dashed off a reply:

Not fair! e-mail me your photo!

She half-anticipated her friend's response:

no way. i never let anyone take my picture.

Lexie understood: Their friendship lived on a mental plane, far above the impermanent world of form, and neither one of them wanted to contaminate it further.

She teased webrider anyway.

liar! never mind. gtg!

The purr of her father's Mercedes-Benz in the driveway sent Lexie flying through the house. Before he had even parked his car, she threw open the garage door and ran to him.

"Did you find it?"

"Yes, I did," he said dryly. Without the slightest hint of excitement, he picked up his metal briefcase, led her into the kitchen, and poured himself a diet iced tea.

Lexie thought she would die from curiosity. "Well?"

He had a strange expression on his face, as if she were a failed genetic experiment. "What?" she said.

"Lexie, how did you know about the letter?"

"I told you. Mom said it was there."

"Uh-huh," was all he said.

After finishing his drink he began once again, in that let's-consider-the-options tone he used to "discuss" things with her. "It wouldn't have been like your mother to tell you about that letter before she died. You have to tell me the truth now. What are you up to?"

"I told you the truth!"

"There has to be a reasonable explanation!"

"There is!"

"It's not possible! You know the video was blank."

"A technical glitch." She hoped, anyway.

They both caught their breath.

"Help me out here," he said. "I'm trying to understand."

Lexie took a deep breath. She had been given another chance. Intention, persistence, and surrender, she reminded herself, would allow her to piggyback on the cosmic energy train and reach her goal in the best way possible. She was demanding that her father accept the truth on her terms. She had to surrender to the path of least resistance. Let him discover the truth for himself; let the Master Programmer do its thing.

"Dad, you don't have to understand."

"All right, Lexie," he said with a sigh.

He finally opened the briefcase and handed over a cream-colored envelope addressed to her in her mother's handwriting.

Lexie pressed the envelope between her palms, savoring the promise of its contents. She longed to read it but would wait as long as she could; there wouldn't be another letter.

Her father, she noticed, had visibly softened as she had backed off. It was one more sign that if she didn't try to control everything, and just let the e-powers configure all the peripherals, she would be just fine. After all, she had been allowed to penetrate the celestial firewall for an obvious and logical reason: to bring her mother's killer to justice. The Master Powers would not have initiated her into the Virtual Believers' Club unless they planned on giving her the tools she needed to accomplish her mission. And right now she needed her dad's help.

"Dad," she said, trying not to gloat. "Remember your promise."

"And just what am I supposed to say to the police?"

"Just ask them to reopen the case."

He nodded. "A deal's a deal."

A quick B-scan revealed her father's new strategy: *Play along with Lexie. Indulge her whims, and maybe she'll stop this childish nonsense.* But she was beginning to understand that there were Higher Energies at work, even if her dad didn't know he was in their service. At least he was pretending to listen. Someday, she hoped, he would get it.

Dad puts on a pair of reality-enhancing 3-D glasses. Startled, he sees subtle golden waves of energy weaving a web all around him, through his body, the house, the trees, rising up from the earth, expanding into the sky, everywhere, in everything and every person. Dad and I are finally connected.

She heard Jane's car pull up outside as her father dialed the phone. *Ugh, her again.*

"Detective Blackwell, please," he said. Lexie shifted her weight back and forth on her feet, waiting.

"Hello!" Miss Perfect Barbie bounced in. "I made you two a barbecued chicken pizza," she said, setting a warm dish on the counter. Oblivious to the tension in the room, she started banging around the kitchen until Lexie's father held up a finger to quiet the idiot.

"Yes, hello, it's David Diamond. I, uh . . ." He paused to clear his throat and shot Lexie an uncomfortable glance. "Detective, I was wondering what it would take for you to reopen my wife's case?

"Yes, sir, I understand." His brow knitted, and he tried to concentrate while Lexie waved a copy of the patient list in his face.

"You see, my daughter hacked her way into my wife's coded patient list. She thought it might lead to . . . yes, I'll tell her." He hung up the phone, avoiding Lexie's searching gaze.

"They see no reason to reopen the case without hard evidence," he said. "However, he'll file the list if we give it to him."

174

What good were grown-ups if they couldn't even get other grown-ups to listen?

"But, Dad—"

He cut her off. "What do you want me to do? Tell them you heard it from your mom?"

Brick by brick, Lexie could feel the invisible wall that separated them being tapped back in place. For a nanosecond, she had thought they could be friends again, but she was wrong. *Friends listen.*

She stuck a Post-it on the patient list that read: *The clue to the real killer is on this list!* With a scornful look, she handed it to her father.

"Will you at least give it to him?" she said.

"Lexie, a thorough investigation was already done."

"Yeah, well, they didn't have Mom helping them."

Exasperated, her father threw up his hands. "Fine, I'll get it to him. But you're not allowed to bother any of these patients. Understand?"

Lexie nodded up, sideways. "Whatever."

"Lexie!"

The sense of injustice that had been festering in her for many months since her mom had left exploded like a tidal wave of anger. "All right, okay! I'm just looking for an answer! No one else is. At least I care."

For a moment, their eyes were locked onto each other until her father looked away. He stared at a cluster of framed family photos on the bulletin board and, keeping his gaze focused there, he said, "You know I care."

"Then prove it," she said. "The police are wrong. We have to find out who did this to Mom."

"Okay," he said, glancing toward the ceiling. "Any suggestions from Up There?"

"All we have is the file of patient code names. We have to study it for clues. Then maybe we can force the police to do something."

He turned toward her and spoke in that this-is-more-serious-than-you-know tone. "All right, but absolutely no contact with any of them. Agreed?"

At least it was a start. "Yeah," she said once again with a vague nod.

She turned to leave when Jane offered her a slice of the warm pizza. At this point, Lexie thought she had better control of the situation and felt more able to tolerate Jane, so she took a big slice.

"Thanks," she said, heading back to her sanctuary. But the urgency in Jane's voice stopped her at the bottom of the stairs, and she tiptoed back to eavesdrop.

"Don't you think it's a little dangerous to keep encouraging her?" she said.

"I know it sounds crazy," her father said. "However, she seems to need to believe that she is connecting to . . . something."

"Well, you don't think that she can actually contact her mother, do you? Honestly, what else can this be but Lexie's over-active *imagination* at work?"

Lexie winced. Predictably, Jane had relied on the explanation she hated most.

"Of course," he said. "But . . . I have to be there for her now."

Lexie smiled. Even if her dad didn't believe her, at least he was on her side.

"But, darling," Jane said. "Have you considered how Lexie will feel when this silly computer fantasy falls apart? She'll only be worse off. I'm terribly worried about her."

"Don't worry. I just have to be there for her now," he repeated with a firm that's-the-end-of-this-discussion tone that Lexie knew well.

But his subtle commands had little effect on Jane. Her voice softened with that feathery sound she often used to trick Lexie's dad. "You did your best, sweetheart," she told him. "You said it yourself: Grace's death had nothing to do with you leaving. It was an accident. Please, David"—now she was nearly whining, like a sick kitten—"stop this nonsense."

Lexie could hear her father sigh. "Lexie needs to get through this her own way. She'll stop when she realizes it's all in her head."

Lexie crept up the stairs and met Ajna-Mac with a wondering glance. *Hey, old friend, are we just a couple of freaks?* But her mother's letter was more potent than any Posball, and the feel of it in Lexie's hand countered her father's and Jane's nasty Negballs. She curled up next to her computer and began reading:

Dear Lexie,
There may have been times when you thought I was too hard on you, or that I didn't care enough. And if I ever failed you, it was only from a lack of skills to teach you the things I wanted you to learn and not from a lack of love. You were created with love and you are deeply loved. Never forget that! Follow your dreams and never let them go. They will guide you to fulfill your life and find the happiness that I wish for you. I followed mine and found true joy in being your mother.
I will always love you,
Mom

Tears rolled down Lexie's cheeks. She quietly folded the letter and tucked it into her desk drawer. If it was the last thing she did, she would avenge her mother's death.

D URING EVERY FREE moment away from school the following week, Lexie scrolled through the patient code list. By Friday, she had almost memorized the data. Secretly she wished Jane's name were there. Oh, how convenient it would be to pin the crime on her. But no matter how hard she projected Jane's name onto the list, Lexie knew she was only fooling herself.

As she studied the list, she let her eyes float over the patients' names, like a general surveying the entire battlefield rather than a single skirmish. Her attention went global, the screen blurred as if seen through the airy dimension into which Lexie was expanding, and the code names formed into a mass of meaningless black marks. And still the name she sought remained a mystery. She rubbed her tired eyes and wondered what she was doing wrong.

C'mon, Ajna-Mac, take me home.

But her e-confessor simply gave her a blank stare. She sat still, waiting—for what she didn't know—just waiting. As she relaxed, she drifted to the calm part of her mind where clarity abounded. In that deep place, she realized she had been tuned to only one channel: the dull beat that reverberated out of her pain. Now that was emotional interference. If she could loosen up and let in whatever came, she might find what she needed. She recalled how good it felt to be in the groove, surfing across the waves—not just on the Web, but in life. Then she would often tingle with satisfaction as life's clues floated toward her with ease. Why was she working so hard to control everything?

INCORRECT: I desperately cling to a swaying buoy, tossed about in a raging sea full of packages. Each box is marked with a tag that reads: CLUE 1, CLUE 2, CLUE 3. *I reach for them in vain, slashing my arm through howling wind, but the clues bob on the whitecaps, beyond my grasp.*
CORRECT: I am lying on the beach, warm and relaxed. Dancing in the calm ocean, the same tagged packages are lined up in a row. A seagull flies overhead, signaling me to attention with its call. Moving in perfect synchronicity with the rolling ocean, I walk toward its edge. The perfect clue is deposited at my feet.

Intention, persistence, surrender, she reminded herself. She had been acting like any other common garden-variety human. Her emotional desperation to unravel the past had tethered her to the Bubble like a dog on a leash. All she had to do was slip into the flow, like the great surfer she was, and catch the Universal Wave. She visualized herself finding the answer. *Yes!* She could see herself doing it. In her mind her desire had already become a reality. For sure, the missing clue would soon come to her— no, strike that thought—it was coming *right now!*

For a little backup, just in case, she pulled up her mom's empty website and wrote: Mom, help!

From far away, perhaps deep inside her mother's website, she thought she heard a horse whinny. She peered into the screen and swore she saw the shadow of a large winged horse fly past.

A winged horse shakes his head, inviting me to fly off into the heavens. I leap onto his silvery back, and we soar through the misty clouds, higher and higher, until we reach a clearing in the snowcapped mountains. He descends upon a ledge and gently lets me down. I approach a low, dark cave where an old man sits cross-legged. His wise eyes greet me as if he knows me.

"Take the path."

"But where is it?"

"Right in front of you. Just keep going."

The mountain begins to shake with a loud banging noise. I fall over the side and grip the ledge. My arms grow weak, but I am unafraid. The rumbling intensifies, my hands slip free, and I plunge through the clouds. . . .

Back into her desk chair? With a jolt, Lexie realized someone was knocking at her door.

Wise old man? Was that the patient code she needed?

Her father opened the door. "Lexie!" he said, pulling her back from the far reaches of her awareness. "Let's go to DiDio's."

"Huh?"

In a daze, as if she had been wrapped in a time warp, she watched her father walk toward her. How long had she been sitting at her desk? She touched her dinner on a tray: cold as ice. Her father waved his hand in front of Ajna-Mac's screen, blocking her view.

"Come with me," he said, his voice robotlike. "A blue raspberry ice. You want it. It is your favorite. Your computer will be here when you return."

Lexie smiled. He was such a dork sometimes. "Okay," she said. She needed to fuel up before she could process another single datum. Anyway, she was always up for a trip to her favorite candy store.

With scissorlike movements, her father lifted her out of the chair. "You will follow me."

"Dad, you're so weird."

"I-AM-WEIRD," he continued in his robotic voice.

They laughed easily together, like before all the problems had started.

At the door, they met Jane, and Lexie stopped, suddenly wary of another threesome outing. To her relief, Jane said,

"Bye, Lexie, see you tomorrow."

"Can't wait, sweetheart," Lexie's father said, then slobbered noisily on Jane's face. Lexie wanted to flee past them, but Jane, as usual, was in her way.

Lexie mumbled, "Bye," then pushed her way past the sick lovebirds out to the front yard, where she inhaled deeply, trying to cleanse herself of their grossness. But she could hear their mushy baby-speak behind her as they walked outside.

Maintaining Dual Focus, she trained her eyes on a nearby tree but saw Jane smile at her. She was so fake. Pretending not to notice, Lexie jumped into her dad's car. After an endless number of nauseating good-byes, her father and Jane drove off in opposite directions. Even the financial news that filled the car, with its numbing monotony of daily facts that Lexie tuned out, was a welcome distraction.

She pulled down the visor mirror and rubbed her nose. A large red spot had popped up right near the tip and was itching like crazy. She sighed, suspecting it was about to erupt into the worst zit she had ever had in her whole life.

Did aliens have zits? *Not.* They probably had some kind of device that permanently zapped them from their bodies: *The Zit Zapper.* I mean, who could imagine an alien's face covered with little flesh-toned blobs or strips of antizit cream? Come to think of it, she had never seen Zoe with a zit. Maybe she was actually a Bubble Spy sent to gather data on earthlings in middle school.

Lexie glanced at her dad, who had a "bearish" look on his

face. "Did Mom have zits when she was growing up?" she said.

His eyes cut over, full of suspicion. "I don't know. Why?" he said.

"Never mind," Lexie said. His B-read bothered her: *What is Lexie trying to prove?* Why couldn't he listen? It was just a simple question. Something she had never asked her mom. There were many other things she wanted to ask her mother now that she couldn't: Had she ever felt invisible? Or hated her own parents?

Her father parked along Montana Avenue, and they walked into the busy candy store. They ordered two blue raspberry ices, and while waiting, her father said, "I believe you're due for a raise in your allowance."

Why did she have this funny feeling that her dad was about to dump something on her?

"I'm proposing a fifteen percent increase," he continued. "That's a lot higher than the cost-of-living index rose last year. What do you think about that?"

"Yeah, whatever," she said.

Now, Lexie had a fine appreciation for the value of money, but according to the law of energy flows, she knew this transfer of power would cost her an equal number of debits. Just what was he after?

Her father held out a pack of red licorice sticks. "Want some Twizzlers for later?"

Whoa, an ice and candy. He was definitely up to something.

"Lexie, I can see that you and Jane are making progress, and that makes me very happy."

So that's it. If she accepted her dad's payoff, instinct told her she would be expected to cancel an equal part of her resistance to Jane's presence in their lives. She was being paid to conform, for God's sake! But as she surveyed the candy-filled shelves—cherry Baby Bottle Pops, Almond Joys, Milk Duds, Jujyfruits—oh man! she was just a kid, and there was so much candy. *More allowance means you could indulge your sweet tooth more often,* her Conformed Self reminded her. She was weak; she admitted it.

She raided the shelves, figuring she might as well cash in while she held the bargaining chip. Her father paid for the ices and her stash. Then, as always, they sat at the bar and dug into their treat, watching the passersby through the large glass window.

After a few minutes, her father said, "I have another proposal, not related, of course. You know, Jane is quite special to me and, well. . . ." He paused, and Lexie held her breath, fearing the worst. "I want her to stay with us for a while, see how—"

Lexie cut him off. "She's moving in?"

He held up a hand, reminding her of a cop trying to prevent an accident. "Not exactly. It's just a trial period. To see how things go. What do you think?"

Lexie's stomach cramped, as if a vise were squeezing her to death. Jane moving into her home? What if she never left? What if she stayed, like, forever? *Oh God, Zoe was right.* All Jane's tricks—the ugly mirrored cap, the cramp pills, the sickeningly sweet concern—were just decoy bonding devices! She had planned to ruin Lexie's life all along.

Lexie's father, his lips stained blue, repeated, "So what do you think?"

Lexie placed her ice on the top of the counter; she wouldn't have another bite. "I think I'd rather die," she said.

Her father just laughed. "Oh, honey, you're so dramatic sometimes. Even you can see what a great contribution Jane is making to our lives."

But all Lexie could see, if Jane was upgraded from a Peripheral Station to a Permanent Link in their family system, was her own demise.

Wandering on a high bodiless frequency through an unending series of doors, I search for my way back—from where, I can't remember, to where, I don't know. More and more each moment, which seems like a year, or maybe a second, I am forgetting, I am forgetting . . . until my entire system defaults and I am no more.

As they drove home Lexie stared out the window, her mood as dark as the violet-blue night sky. She just had to hack this Jane problem.

As soon as her father pulled onto their street, Lexie gasped. She sat at attention, leaning forward as if straining to hear some distant sound. Something was terribly wrong.

"Hurry, Dad!"

"What is it?"

She didn't have to explain. In a few seconds they were in front of their house. The yard was littered with trash, and the front door was ajar.

"Ajna-Mac!" She bolted from the car.

"Lexie, wait!" But she was already inside.

Her heart raced as she flew to her room. She screamed. Ajna-Mac was gone! A second punch to her emotional gut soon followed: Her mother's computer was also missing.

"No!" She wailed till she thought her lungs would burst, though she wouldn't have cared if they had. Slumped over her desk, she sobbed bitter tears at the place where Ajna-Mac had always been. Her primary means of interfacing with life—and perhaps her only conduit to her mother—had been ripped away from her. It was the cruelest violation she could ever imagine. Life in the Bubble was just a series of random events that produced pain and suffering. It totally sucked.

Her father rushed to her side, panting, "Damn thieves, the TVs are gone." He took in Lexie's empty desk. "Oh no. Don't worry, honey, I'll get you a new computer."

"You don't understand." *Disconnected.* From her computer. Her father. Her mother. Even herself. Her life was over! *That's right,* her Conformed Self sneered. *Beep, time's up, you lose. Deposit another life if you want to try again.* Her words, barely audible, fell from her lips like heavy stones. "You—just—don't—understand."

Her father wasn't listening anyway. "I'd better call the police. Where's that insurance number?" he said, hurrying away.

Just then, a searing pain shot through her belly. *Oh, great.* As if in a trance she walked to her bathroom and pulled out the dreaded box of tampons. She sank down against the side of the tub, depressed by the calculations that were running through her head: unless a gender-equalizing pill was invented in the near future, she could expect at least four or five miserable days every month for probably another thirty-five years! She grabbed a calculator and her eyes widened as she punched in the hopeless numbers: She was trapped for at least another 1,680 more days!

And neither her mom nor Ajna-Mac could console her now.

D ESPERATE TO RECONNECT with her mother, the
Web, or anything that existed in a dimension outside of
the Bubble, Lexie skipped her first class Monday morning and snuck into the empty computer lab. As soon as she
landed online, she sent webrider the following e-mail:

> hemorrhaging freedom here. my soul has been
> ripped out, right down to the hardware—gone!
> maybe my portal was discovered and THEY sent
> someone to steal my computer. i hope to connect
> soon, but don't know when. keep the faith for me.

Skipping over to virtualbelievers.com, she reassured herself
that, any minute, her mom would dial in and tell her what to do.
She bit her already ragged nails while waiting for her mother's
website to appear.

Empty.

She sat with her head in her hands, wondering once again if there was a magical key that gave her access to the Beyond. Although she practiced intention, persistence, and surrender, she still felt the lack of something in her. Perhaps, she worried, Ajna-Mac was the missing link. With him gone, she might never see her mother again. Dissatisfied, she signed off and hurried away from the sight of all those computers, which only made her heart ache for her e-Master.

The day passed in a numb haze, and later that afternoon, with no visible display of emotion, she recorded the fact that Jane was moving several boxes and suitcases into Lexie's house. And without Ajna-Mac as an emotional outlet, her confusion and stress went stratospheric. She felt cyberparalyzed, netdead. She disappeared into her room and sat at her desk in a semi-trance, staring at the vacant spot Ajna-Mac had occupied. It was all she could do. She ate peanut butter from the jar, and no matter what anyone said to her, she simply replied, "Whatever."

The following Saturday morning her father and Jane appeared uninvited in her room, both smiling as if they shared some stupid secret.

"Hi, honey," her father said, using his optimistic voice. "C'mon smile, it's a beautiful day." Slumped over her lonely desktop, Lexie ignored him.

"Don't you think it's a great day for horseback riding?" Jane asked her.

"Whatever," Lexie said. *Where did Dad find this Nature Barbie anyway?*

"Jane is an expert horsewoman," he said, his chest puffing with pride. "She's offered to give you some lessons."

Were they talking to *her*? She was dying here, and they were talking about an adventurous playdate. She turned to see her father pick up her backpack as if there might be a bomb inside waiting to trigger Lexie's own explosion. When he caught her staring at him, he took a step backward, and his B-thoughts couldn't have hurt her more deeply than if he had said them out loud: *Lexie is like a wild animal. She might do something unpredictable—jump out of her window, or even attack me. Be careful.*

It didn't matter. She was reconciled to the fact that he would probably never understand her again as he had when she was young.

"You can't spend the rest of your life locked up in here," Jane said.

Lexie wasn't fooled. She bet Jane was happy that "this nonsense" had ended. With the focus off the search for Lexie's mother's killer, Jane had Lexie's dad all to herself now.

"Jane's absolutely right," her father said, handing over Lexie's backpack to her. Lexie was about to protest when her father lifted her by both arms and led her out of the room.

"Leave me alone!" she said in vain.

"It's a pity how little advantage you take of living in sunny Southern California. Start making an effort, and I'll see what I

191

can do about getting you a new computer."

Lexie was no match for her dad's strength and decided to zone out until he tired of improving her life, which she hoped would be soon. At least she might finally get back online.

They headed outside, and he dumped her into Jane's Jeep. Jane slipped behind the steering wheel and smiled at her. "Ready?"

"Hey! What's going on?" Lexie said as her father shut her in the car.

"Have fun, girls."

Lexie slumped against the car door and pressed her forehead against the window frame. *Whatever.*

As they drove down the street, she saw Wilson riding his skateboard on the sidewalk, his long blond hair sailing behind him, his tall strong body balanced with ease. Again she wondered about the simplicity of his ways. Did it bother him that they were prisoners on some waterlogged planet rocketing on autopilot through a third-rate galaxy? Did his emotions ever pull him down into a bottomless pit of despair, or was he actually as carefree as he seemed?

As their eyes met, however, she was touched by an unexpected tenderness. She could almost swear that he was concerned about her. But why would he be? *Now* she was really imagining things.

Then he smiled at her like he had once before, and Lexie felt the warmth of his genuineness spread through her as rapidly as one of those sweet, feel-good chain e-mails. For a moment she forgot the ruin of her life; there was only Wilson's amazing smile. This time she shyly returned his smile before he disappeared from view as the Jeep turned the corner.

"Is that your boyfriend?" Jane said, shattering Lexie's mellow high.

She shot Jane an angry look. "N-o-o!" Since Jane couldn't possibly have been serious, Lexie assumed she was making terrible fun of her.

"Why not? He's cute."

What is the point of communicating with an alien?

They sped down Pacific Coast Highway in silence. Lexie watched the cars passing by, each filled with such happy-looking people. Was she the only miserable person on the West Coast? Perhaps Karma Kong had made a big mistake with her life. Or perhaps she was paying off a debt for having committed some horrible, forgotten deed in the past. She carefully scrolled through her Internal Memory, watching her life as if it were a movie starring someone else, but could not find any transgression worthy of such brutal payback.

Round and round I go, belted onto the Wheel of Life, which spins out to infinity, like a crazy amusement park ride. As I circle into my current life, a random trigger activates a jet spray, and I'm covered with a special dye. This marks me as easy pickings to any passing alien troublemaker. It means my life will be hell.

Jane turned onto Topanga Canyon Road, and they snaked up the steep road through the chaparral-covered mountains. After a while, she pulled onto a dirt road that led to a small barn.

"Here we are," she said. She grabbed a riding crop from the back of the Jeep and hopped out. Lexie put her feet up on the dashboard, settling in.

Jane looked at her expectantly. "Aren't you coming?" Lexie closed her eyes. "All right then," Jane said.

Lexie peeked to see her walk to a fenced-in pen where a Wild West dude wearing a frayed cowboy hat was brushing down a large, brown horse. They chatted while Jane stroked the beast's nose—for sure, a dangerous, dumb thing to do.

Jane turned suddenly, catching Lexie's gaze. "C'mon," she said. "You can't sit in the car all day."

Still Lexie didn't budge. She was on Pause, and she had no intention of resuming Play—not here, not with her, no way.

"Well, I'm going for a ride. You can stay if you want to, but don't wander off by yourself. There are coyotes and mountain lions in these parts."

Coyotes and mountain lions? Lexie jumped out of the car and raced to the barn.

Jane smiled coyly. "Changed your mind?"

Up close, Lexie caught a whiff of the cowboy's body odor, a foul mixture of sweat, beer, and some other things she didn't even want to think about. She lurched away, right into a pile of horse manure.

The cowboy spit on the ground. "Looks like you got the prize, girlie." Then he walked inside the barn.

Lexie scraped her Nikes clean on the grass. She hated being outdoors.

"Here," Jane said, offering her a sugar cube. "Why don't you make friends with Lucky? Give him a treat."

"Are you insane?" Lexie said.

According to her way of thinking, if you couldn't unplug it, you shouldn't touch it. Power sources should be manageable, logical. This monster was one massive heap of wild mega-energy with no On/Off button. Interfacing with it was not an option!

Jane laughed her irritating, fake homespun laugh. "If you're calm," she said, "Lucky will be, too. Don't be such a scaredy-cat." She thrust the small cube into Lexie's palm. "This is life, not some computer game. C'mon, try."

Lexie was learning that sometimes the Universe had a bizarre way of sending her messages. As she stared at the slimy saliva gurgling out of the horse's mouth, it occurred to her that this unexpected outing might offer her some new insight. Why else would the Master Game Player contrive to place her in such foreign territory, if not to reveal some unimaginable clue that could only be detected under these strange circumstances? *Ride the wave.* Perhaps if she dealt with Lucky, she would pass her next lesson and reach a Higher Level.

"Okay!" she said, trying to sound enthusiastic.

Jane beamed. "Attagirl!"

Planting her feet in the dirt, Lexie braced her arm, holding it out like a statue. The horse, who was several feet away, bared its teeth and dove like some crazed sugar addict right at her. Lexie screamed and jumped three feet back.

"Silly," Jane said, without malice. "Let me help you."

Holding Lexie's arm, she drew her close to the fence and guided her toward the animal's mouth. "Just relax," she said, shaking out Lexie's stiffness. "I won't let anything happen to you." Then she made a little clicking noise to the horse, which Lexie hoped didn't mean *Bite the nerd.*

Flow, don't resist, Lexie reminded herself. She closed her eyes and felt the soft wetness from the horse's muzzle dripping into her hand. She was inside the event now, not separate, and because she was a part of it, the experience held no more fear. She opened her eyes. The sugar cube was gone!

"Cool," she said, barely managing to conceal her delight.

Jane bounced up and down, her long curls like springs. "Congratulations! I knew you could do it."

Wow, that was like a bonding thing, wasn't it? Was it possible that she had been entirely wrong about Jane? Was that the message in her Personal Mailbox? With her perceptors on full alert, she checked out Jane's Monitor B and was floored by its relatively benign content: *Since I have to deal with Lexie, I might as well make the best of it.* For an escaped alien like Jane, that wasn't bad.

The cowboy walked back to them, leading two horses. "Are

196

these the ones you wanted, ma'am?"

"Yep, thanks," Jane said, taking the reins. She cooed to the horses as she led them down a dusty trail. "C'mon, cowgirl, follow me," she told Lexie.

Why not? Lexie kept a safe distance behind. They walked for several yards, stopping behind a large clump of bushes.

"Just remember to relax and you'll be fine, I promise," Jane said. She bent down next to one of the horses and cupped her hands together. "Step up."

Up there? Lexie's eyes traveled the length of the huge animal. What was she thinking? This was insane; she didn't belong in the wild. She belonged in an electronically controlled environment. An overwhelming urge to run for her life seized her.

Jane reached for her hand just as she was about to flee. "It's okay," she said.

Her touch was so reassuring. Encouraged by her recent success in the Game of Life, Lexie squelched her panic and let Jane boost her up into the saddle. But as the ground receded, far, far away, spinning like the Ferris wheel at the pier, she clutched the leather stump thingy in front of her and cursed her malfunctioning logic. Like her dad, she too must have fallen under Jane's spell.

"Hey, you're a natural!" Jane said, slapping Lexie's thigh just a little too hard. Lexie flinched, and the nonprogammable creature beneath her spun around with a loud whinny.

Lexie screamed, every muscle tightly flexed. "Get me off this thing!"

"Calm down!"

But there was no Calm Option for this program. There was no Escape Key, either.

Jane grabbed Lexie's horse's reins, and the horse quieted, as if by her magic touch. Lexie watched her mount the other horse with ease. She made that clicking sound again and led Lexie along the trail that meandered through the bushy mountainside, carrying her farther away from civilization. And as the rocking of her horse's hips bounced Lexie from side to side in the saddle, she tried to surrender but only felt nauseated.

"See, if you're calm, he'll be calm," Jane said. "Animals respond to what you're feeling. You know, I used to clean stalls when I was your age in exchange for riding lessons, and my horse always sensed my mood. I remember one day, when I was mad as the devil, he took off like lightning the minute he saw me."

Lexie caught a glimpse of Jane's eyes and detected something that made her want to run away, too. She shivered and broke out in a cold sweat.

"Are you okay?" Jane added, as if she had Monitor B'd Lexie.

Lexie nodded yes/no; she was just imagining things. The bumpy ride was distorting her perceptions.

"Maybe your horse had ESP," Lexie said as a joke, trying to shake her growing sense of dread.

To her surprise, Jane agreed. "I think he did." Then she

sighed and added in a young girl's dreamy voice, "Pegasus was a very special horse."

Pegasus? The vision of a winged horse . . . the old man's advice . . . take the path right in front of you. Lexie could barely think straight, her gears were turning so fast. Pegasus, she realized, not a wise old man, was the patient code she needed. Exhilarated, she googled her Internal Memory and thought she recalled a Pegasus on her mother's list of patients. But a sudden streak of Negballs pummeled her into doubting herself. *Jane isn't on the patient list! You're just being paranoid.* This was way too weird! Maybe her dizziness had caused a logic malfunction.

"Um, was Pegasus really important to you?" she asked.

"Definitely." The words floated from Jane's lips. "It felt like we were flying whenever I rode him. I loved him more than anyone in the whole world."

Lexie's systems began to clang, as if a meteor had entered her atmosphere and was about to hit. All she could think was, *I'm stuck on top of a huge, wild beast, and Pegasus is the key to Jane's personality!* Her breath caught in her chest as her mother's words echoed in her head: "Be careful." Had her mom been trying to warn her about *Jane*?

Time-out! Lexie told herself. *Reality check:* She touched the horse, looked at the sky, looked at the trees, looked at Jane. Dad loved Jane. She wanted to be Lexie's friend. She gave her that cute hat. She said no one could replace her mother. She understood. But Lexie couldn't stem the fear. *Sanity check:* Something

199

was very, very wrong here.

"Can I ask you something?" Lexie said, hoping the trotting of the horses' hooves would drown out her pounding heart.

Jane smiled. "Of course, ask me anything."

Yeah, see, Jane wanted to be her friend. "Well, I was just wondering if you ever told my mom about your horse?"

Jane's head gave a little jerk, and a quick B-glance revealed she was hiding something. Lexie had opened the back door to a strange program. She was in! She didn't know where, but she was definitely in.

"No," Jane said, riding the vowel way too long, as if she were trying to block Lexie's entry. "You know I never knew her. Why do you ask?"

"Um, it's hard to explain, but I think Pegasus meant something to my mom, too."

"Really, like what?"

"I'm not sure, but I know it was important."

"Oh, well, I guess you'll never know," she said with a dismissive tone.

A dark cloud passed overhead, and an eerie shadow fell across Jane. The look on her face, which could have killed a small animal, told Lexie she had finally stumbled upon Jane's camouflaged B-screen. Then, as if switching programs, Jane smiled all cheerylike.

"You look pretty good up there for a city slicker! Too bad your dad can't see you."

Access denied! Damn! Lexie was back outside of Jane's mindware.

Then, without warning, Jane changed their course, pushing Lexie's horse down a straight path that led to a high stone wall. If Jane gripped that whipping stick any tighter, it would snap. *Wow, is she tense or what?*

A loud *Crack!* reverberated in the air, and Lexie felt something hit her horse. The beast took off, flying through the air faster than the spaceship of Vega, The Warrior Goddess. Straight ahead she saw the stone wall and realized they were racing toward it! She clung to the neck of the berserk animal. The wall zoomed closer and closer until, with total clarity, she understood that either the wall had to move or she would crash into it.

She screamed for help, but the only reply she thought she heard was Jane's scary laugh in the wind. Terrified, she stared at the stones in the wall, which were getting closer but somehow smaller. Quick computation: *Oh no!* The horse was jumping! In midair, it shook Lexie loose and the ground reached up and grabbed her, banging into her backside with a powerful force.

She lay on the rocky path, moaning in agony. Just then a cool, silent shadow passed in front of her. She opened her eyes and saw Jane walking toward her, the whipping stick at her side. Lexie's mind was whirling as she tried to assemble the disjointed events. She recalled Jane's grip tightening around the stick right before her horse had taken off. All at once, everything made sense.

"Are you insane?" she said. "You hit my horse!"

The sun burst from behind the clouds, forming a perfect orange ring around Jane; her curly hair sizzled like Medusa's. She squinted and raised the riding crop high over her head. Oh my God! Jane was going to finish her off. Lexie buried her head in her chest and threw her arms up to protect herself.

"Help! Help! Somebody help me!"

She hunched over, anticipating Jane's blows, when she heard a horse galloping toward her. Peeking through the crack between her arms, she was relieved to see the cowboy riding toward them.

He called out to her. "Hey! You okay, miss?"

Lexie watched in disbelief as Jane put on a concerned face and morphed into an "upset friend."

"Her horse bolted! Better call a paramedic."

Liar! Lexie pointed a shaking finger at Jane. "She hit my horse! She tried to kill me—"

"What?" Jane said, cutting her off, with a sharp hissing sound. "Something must have startled her horse."

A throbbing pain shot up through Lexie's shoulders, and she wondered why the cowboy was just standing there. Why wasn't he roping Jane up? What was he waiting for, a confession?

Lexie cried. "She was going to whack me with her stick."

"Don't be ridiculous," Jane said, swooshing the riding crop through the air as if it were nothing more than a fairy wand. "I was blocking the sun from my eyes." Her voice rose to a shrill, unearthly pitch. "Look at her, the poor girl is scared silly. I doubt we'll ever get her back in the saddle again. Bad beginner's luck!"

The cowboy shook his head. "Sorry, miss. Never would have put a beginner on that one. He's a jumper."

"A jumper?" Lexie repeated. "Why didn't you say—" Of course, the cowboy hadn't seen her mount the "jumper"! She stared coldly at Jane. "That's why you hid behind those bushes! You didn't want him to see me on the wild horse!"

"Oh for heaven's sake, Lexie! I was trying to save you the embarrassment."

"Yeah, right!"

This "expert horsewoman" had given Lexie, a total gear-head, a "jumper" to ride! Their little rodeo was no coincidence. With that one little clue, Lexie deactivated the blinding virus that had been racing through her, blocking a clear view of Jane. She entered this new data into her JANE file and shuddered as her Internal Analyzer spit out the correct sequence.

To her utter amazement, she realized that her perceptions of Jane had never been dulled by emotional content at all. From that very first day when her bogus meter had gone ballistic at Jane's appearance, to the sudden view of Jane's evil nature on the tennis court, to her growing resistance to Jane, she understood that she had been right about Jane all along. No warped *Motherless Girl Hates Girlfriend* virus had messed with her head.

Instead she was a lone rider programming a path for truth in this mixed-up world.

She was totally plugged in now: *Dad is in love with a psycho.* In fact, she realized with a cold chill that Jane was willing to maim or even kill her if necessary, and quite possibly—the thought struck hard—was somehow connected to her mom's demise. If it was the last thing Lexie did, she would show her father the truth and trash this wicked stepmom wannabe.

L EXIE LEANED AGAINST her father's arm, taking one agonizing step at a time up the stairs. Not for one single instant did she take her mind off Jane's quiet, lethal presence behind them. As they entered Lexie's bedroom, the Evil One rushed ahead to arrange the bed pillows, but Lexie repelled her with an indignant stare. Lexie's father, in turn, shot Lexie a warning glance as he eased her onto the bed. Jane then sent an urgent semaphore to Lexie's father: *Help!* At some other time, Lexie might have been amused by this roundelay of B-telegraphs, but for now she was focused on her mission to expose Jane. It began like this: *Let the criminal build her own trap.*

"I'm so sorry, Lexie," Jane said, sucking in her breath. "I wanted you to have a good experience. I thought you'd enjoy a more spirited horse; there's nothing worse than a dull ride. Of course, I never dreamed he'd jump." She sighed and batted her pleading eyes at Lexie's father. As Lexie expected, he came to Jane's initial defense.

"The horse reacted to Lexie's fear," he said. "It wasn't your fault, sweetheart. Lexie understands that; she's just upset."

Lexie didn't protest. She wasn't on the defensive, but she wasn't on the offensive, either. She was in no hurry. Confident of what she knew, she was waiting to be alone with her dad. All she had to do was deliver the facts. If she held on through the storm of lies that Jane was sure to unleash, she trusted that she would eventually win the game. Jane would soon be history. And now, the closer the time came for their little showdown, the more nervous Jane seemed. Lexie was even beginning to enjoy the little tics and jittery air that Jane gave off like an animal in danger.

"I hope you'll give me another chance," Jane said.

"Of course she will," Lexie's father said, sending Lexie another threatening telegraph. But she buried her face in a magazine, ignoring them both. "Why don't you go relax?" he told Jane.

Yeah, get lost! Her dad was a fair guy, and she knew he was waiting to hear her side of the story. The second that Jane's tiny butt hit the hallway, Lexie would lay it out for him to see.

Jane wrung her hands. "Well, good night then. Can I get you anything before I go?"

Lexie almost laughed at Jane's Bambi stare. When would

adults learn that you couldn't fake your feelings? Real feelings were the only thing that separated the human pets from the small, brave tribe of The Unconformed who refused to be tamed.

"Lexie?" her dad said. But Lexie didn't respond. He gave a frustrated nod to Jane, who left the room at last. Then he closed the door and stood staring at it for a moment. Lexie could hear him taking a deep breath.

"Dad—" she began. But he whirled around, his face pinched with anger.

"What is wrong with you?"

"Dad, listen!" It would be more difficult to get him to focus than she had thought. She jettisoned her well-planned attack and blurted out the facts. "Jane attacked me! She made me ride this wild 'jumper horse' on purpose! Then she whacked it so hard it took off like the Road Runner. She knew I would fall off when it jumped." Lexie paused. It had worked. Her dad was in Listen Mode. She looked right at him. No defense. No anger. She wanted him to look into her Real Self's eyes and remember that she was his daughter, not an alien. With as much calmness as she could muster, she delivered the most obvious conclusion: "She tried to kill me."

Her father whistled with sarcasm, and she realized she had mistaken his listening for the usual act of judging her. There was a fine line between the two modes in grown-ups.

"Wait a minute!" he said. "You're way out of line here. How can you even suggest that Jane would try, or even want, to harm you?"

Am I the one on trial here, or what? She reminded herself to be patient with him; he was still under Jane's spell. "Dad," she said, imitating Adult Speak with extra emphasis on each syllable, "Jane hit my horse with her riding crop; it wasn't an accident."

"I don't suppose you actually *saw* her hit the horse, did you?"

"I didn't have to see her, I *know* she did it!"

"C'mon, Lexie, you're a smart kid, you know you can't accuse someone of hurting you just because you imagined it. Anything could have set off that horse."

Imagine! Imagine? But she refused to doubt herself this time. She had indisputable facts!

"But I *heard* her smack my horse and I *felt* it!"

"Think, Lexie! Isn't it just possible that something could have fallen on the horse? Isn't it?"

"No! It came from Jane's direction. And if that cowboy hadn't come along, she would have hit me, too!"

Her father shook his head in disgust, and Lexie feared he was giving up on her. "Jane has bent over backward to make this work," he said. "She's the sweetest, most considerate person in the world, and she thinks you hate her."

"I do. I wish she would just leave." Lexie hadn't meant to expose her deepest feelings, especially not now, when he seemed to have abandoned her, but he was her dad, after all, and she longed to tell him all the truths in her heart.

"Well, Jane is not leaving," he said. "She's staying, so you had better get used to it. I'm counting on you to try and be a little more grown-up about this situation. You're not a child anymore."

Excuse me? But who was acting like a child here? Not the one with the broken back. *Jeez!* Ever since Jane came along, her dad had been lost in space. Zoe was right; he didn't believe a word she said about Jane. Even worse, she could tell by the cool chill now emanating from his Monitor B that, by exposing her true feelings, she had indeed lost any advantage she once had. *Courage,* she told herself; she still had hard facts to present.

"Dad, Jane's favorite horse was called Pegasus. . . ." She hesitated, but the trembling in her voice never betrayed the conviction in her heart. "And that's a major clue to Mom's killer. Somehow there's a connection to Jane. I know it."

Her father narrowed his eyes. "Okay. You have to stop all this nonsense now. Or else . . ." He studied her for a moment and then continued in a measured tone. "Or else, I'm afraid we'll have to come up with some alternate arrangements."

Zoe, she unhappily recalled, had also predicted Lexie would be banished to a dreaded boarding school if she couldn't deal with the Step. With her fears inflamed, she pressed on. She had no choice, no matter what the cost—her home, her father, even her life!

"Just take a look," Lexie said. "I gave you a hard copy of the list. Do you still have it? Just look and see if Pegasus is listed as a code." And then she did something she despised. She resorted to the most common grown-up tactic: manipulation. "Or are you afraid to look? I mean, if I'm wrong, then there won't be a Pegasus on the list, will there? At least then you can convince me and I'll stop bugging you."

Her father heaved a weary sigh. "Lexie, please, this isn't necessary."

"No, Dad, really, I'm not afraid to be wrong. Just get the list."

For a moment they looked at each other, and she detected a wave of sorrow flowing through him. Poor Dad, sometimes she too wished she hadn't been born.

"All right," he said, at last. "You win. I'll be right back."

Lexie slumped back on the bed, exhausted from their fight. She could hear her father's footsteps as he went downstairs, and she thought she heard a hushed argument between him and Jane. A wild thought occurred to her: Maybe Jane would give up on the boyfriend with the crazy kid. But when her dad returned, looking as determined as ever, she knew it was just a fantasy.

He sat straight in her desk chair and crossed his legs as if he were about to begin a business meeting. "Now, Lexie," he said, "I've been very patient with you, and God knows I've tried my best, but I am not kidding. This is the last time I will indulge you." He held up the list. "No Jane listed here, no more story. Once and for all, we end this . . . this thing you're doing. You promise to behave with Jane and deal with the past in a more normal way. Is it a deal?"

If Lexie had been outside herself, watching herself and her dad, she might have thought she was taking a roll of the dice. After all, she had been proven wrong already with the missing footage of her mom's supposed appearance. And she hadn't seen her mother since then, either. The apparent odds were not in her favor. But she had come a long way since this story began, and although she recognized the way things looked on the outside, a concurrent awareness of her inner life had grown to the point where she was able to say, "No problem, Dad, just read it." She knew she had nothing to fear. *Let it come,* she told herself. *And enjoy the ride.*

Her father pulled a pair of reading glasses from his shirt pocket and flexed the paper in his hand. "Let's see. *M, N,* Oscars, here we are *P, Papillon.*" He glanced at Lexie as he paused to flip the page. "You okay?" he said. She gave him a quick, ambiguous nod; she would be okay once he convicted Jane.

"Okay," he said, with a resigned air. "Puppy, Patchouli, and . . ." All of a sudden, it happened. Both his Monitor A and B registered mega-disappointment. "Pegasus," he said, his voice dropping. Neither said a word as their eyes met in brief acknowledgment of the discovery. Her father continued, scanning across the page. "Well, you were right. One of her patients was crazier than the rest."

"Jane?"

"No, Lexie," he said in a calm voice. "John Simpson's girlfriend, Susan Butler. The woman who killed your mother." He glanced at the list. "Diagnosis: paranoid schizophrenic."

"No way!" Lexie hobbled over and grabbed the list from his hand. But it was just as he said. "Ugh!"

"The driver of the car that hit your mother was one of her patients; it just confirms that she did it. Paranoid schizophrenics live in a world of altered reality. In other words, they're insane."

To her father's credit he didn't gloat. He waited until she had ripped up the pages, dumped them in the wastebasket, and eased herself back onto the bed. He patted her head as if she were a good pet and said, "You'll feel better in the morning." Then he left her alone.

Up to that moment, Lexie had truly believed she was not a child of the Bubble, although she wasn't an alien, either. She suspected that her true identity hung somewhere outside of the known possibilities. Yet the odd pieces of her unique programming were forming together in her mind over time. She had even developed a sort of comfort zone within this thing called "Lexie."

Now there was only one thing that would redeem her sense of self and perhaps help her find some meaning in this miserable Bubble: She had to prove her case against Jane.

I am trapped, chained inside Jane's monstrous computer. Stripped of her human costume, she appears as her true self: a mutated alien, half devil, half basilisk. She laughs like a fiend as she reprograms my life. I cry out to my father, but she has corrupted his system with a warped Kid Filter. I struggle to break free; I must not quit. Overload, overload!

THE NEXT MORNING Lexie woke with a sinking feeling in her gut. *You've been dreaming,* her Conformed Self taunted her, *just like you dreamed up the whole JANE/HORSE INCIDENT.* Lexie groaned and covered her head with her pillow, desperate to block out the doubt that inevitably followed her father's accusation of having an overactive imagination.

She rolled over in the bed, careful to avoid the ache in her back, and stared at the silicon chip mobile gently twisting in the breeze. Her mother's words echoed in her thoughts: *Just believe in yourself . . . you already have everything you need to find your way.* She replayed the JANE/HORSE INCIDENT over and over on her Inner Screen, attempting to view it as logically as possible, as if she were seeing it through her father's eyes. And each time she became more convinced of Jane's malevolence, until at last she had purified herself of all her father's Negballs and was able to tap into the simplicity of pure Lexieware.

She reconsidered her case against Jane. In her gut she knew Jane was guilty of trying to destroy her. The logical sequence in her mind pointed, therefore, to Jane as the main suspect in Lexie's mother's death. But Lexie's word wasn't good enough for her dad or the police. Ethereally channeled clues, like Pegasus, just didn't cut it in the sensitivity-clogged Bubble. For God's sake, her own near demise—twice!—at Jane's hands had only been an opportunity for her father to be even nicer to the Witch. What she needed was tangible evidence that linked Jane to Lexie's mother or revealed some damaging secrets about her past.

Let it come, her Real Self reminded her. But how could she surrender to the flow when her own life might be in danger? The Universe would have to step up, and fast.

She was so distracted by her thoughts that a knock at the door made her jump.

"Lexie, are you all right?" her dad called out.

"Yeah, why wouldn't I be?" she said, opting for nonchalance.

There was a pause, and she figured he had to switch gears. Good, keep him off balance.

He pushed the door open and peeked in. "Want to go for a Sunday drive with us?"

"Maybe next time. I'm busy."

"Doing what?"

It was worth a hit from Karma Kong: "I'm meeting some friends."

Again her father hesitated and looked at her as if he didn't recognize her. "Oh," he finally said. "Have fun."

"You, too," she said, trying to sound mature, even grown-up.

She waited until she heard the front door slam shut, then scooted to the window to see them drive off in Jane's Jeep.

A perfect spying opportunity.

She dressed and headed downstairs to the guest room, where Jane and her father stayed. A shiver went up Lexie's spine as she entered the room, which was filled with Jane's icky aura. She scanned the room for clues to Jane's secrets, hoping something would point her in the right direction. But the messy clutter of half-open boxes piled willy-nilly and clothes strewn around the room distorted her signals. It figured: Little Miss Perfect meets Total Chaos. God, Dad had to be in love. How else could he live like that?

Lexie's senses, on super alert now, were up to the task. She wandered about, relying on her Internal Radar to guide her toward the subtle, glowing energy that surrounded a clue.

A music box of a porcelain mother rocking a baby, a cherished knickknack Lexie's mom had used to decorate the guest room, caught her eye from behind the heaps of junk on the dresser. On impulse, she picked it up and wound the music key: *Twinkle, twinkle, little star.* . . . She recalled her mom singing that very

216

tune to her many times. She could hear her gentle voice, "Which star looks like a diamond in the sky?" And she smiled as she pictured her own freshly bathed, pruney little hand, pointing at the first star of the night. For a second, she felt the joy of picking just the right star as her mother hugged her and said, "I love you, Shiny Diamond." With a wistful sigh, Lexie put the music box back in its place, more determined than ever to discover the mystery of her mother's untimely departure.

She studied the room again. The closet door was ajar, and she felt the telltale tingle of a clue. She picked her way across the room, careful not to disturb the piles of dirty laundry, and slipped inside. As soon as she turned on the overhead light, Jane's tacky, faux needlepoint suitcases went 3-D. She examined the clean, unmarked cases up close and sneezed, overpowered by the brand-new smell of the fabric. No way had any of this luggage ever been to India, Australia, or anywhere else that Jane bragged about traveling to on her "catalog job"! For God's sake, she probably didn't even have a job.

But Lexie's Conformed Self pointed out that, of course, the luggage might have been a recent purchase. Lexie paused to consider that possibility, but her B-senses were buzzing with such intensity that she discarded it.

She unzipped the largest case: A clue was coming! She rummaged through the interior pockets. *Hold on, here it comes!* She sensed that something was about to float over the virtual wave she was surfing. She could almost feel the cool water running over her hand as she reached to pick it up—but the pockets were all empty.

Narrowing her focus, she realized her perceptors were burning into the small carry-on case. She flung it open and glided into the bottom pocket. She finally connected. *YES!* An outrageous clue: an American passport! At last, something that might expose Jane's trickery. You couldn't lie on your passport.

Suddenly, she heard the front door slam again. She froze. She was beyond dead! *Please let it be Dad!*

Rapid footsteps were approaching in the hallway. She scrambled to stuff the passport back in its place and zip up the suitcases, rearranging them as best she could. She hid behind the largest one and held her breath . . . *Twinkle, twinkle, little star. . . . Oh no!* The music box was still playing!

She heard someone enter the room and peered past the edge of the suitcase, staring through the crack in the doorjamb: *Jane!* And Lexie detected no Dad vibe in the house to protect her, either. She'd been tricked. Jane must have dropped him somewhere and circled back.

Lexie watched, wide-eyed, as Jane examined the music box, then cast a suspicious glance around the room. Desperate not to emit any detectable vibes, Lexie almost lost the struggle when she picked up Jane's Shadow-thoughts: *I bet Lexie has been here . . . and maybe the little jerk is still around.*

With increasing horror, she saw Jane drop to her knees and look under the bed. Lexie squirmed in the deadly stillness as

Jane rose to her feet and clapped the dust from her hands. Then, like an arrow that pierced Lexie's heart, Jane's eyes darted over to the closet. *Yikes!* She was heading toward it. *Make like a yogi!* Lexie told herself, folding into a pretzel-like shape.

Time had looped in a figure eight; she was living out a childhood nightmare.

I am lying very, very still in my bed, clutching the sheet to my chin. In the distance, I see a huge thing, a sort of dinosaur-gorilla crashing toward me. The monster tracks my scent as it races through my neighborhood, pounding the ground louder and louder. It knocks over buildings as if they were toys, filling the air with its terrifying roar. I can see it clearly now. I'll be dead soon. Its jagged teeth shine in the moonlight. Its bloodshot eyes look right through my window. Oh no! It rips off the roof. A gigantic hand grabs me. I scream. . . .

Don't sneeze, don't cough, don't breathe! Lexie warned herself. But like a tightrope walker swaying on the edge, she feared she would lose control any second. Here she was, trapped in the guest closet, while an insane woman—with whom her dad was madly in love—poked at some dry cleaning bags, unaware of Lexie's nearby presence. The absurdity of her situation caused ripples of nervous, quiet laughter to tickle her. As it threatened to erupt, she held her body as rigid as possible, dreading her own rebelliousness. She would be in exile for months, maybe years, if Dad heard about this.

Despite her efforts, however, a giggle bubble burst in her brain and was on a rapid trajectory toward her mouth, about to explode, when she heard the sound of Jane's footsteps in the hallway.

"Lexie?" Jane called out.

Lexie resumed her viewing position just as Jane returned. She saw her lock the door behind her, and then, with a shrug, toss the music box into a metal wastebasket. It landed with a shattering *Crash!* Lexie stifled a scream. Violent anger pumped through her body. She had never hated anyone or anything as much as she hated Jane. Only a sick, vicious alien would destroy her mother's old music box.

But the sight of Jane counting out a huge pile of money short-circuited her rage. Wow, she had a lot of cash. She had to be a real criminal. Lexie watched as she stuffed a packet of money into her purse. What was she going to do with all that loot? Lexie's Real Self considered sticking her head out of the closet and simply asking her. She pictured Jane's horrified reaction, caught in some illegal act, and once more Lexie fell into an uncontrollable silly fit. Just as Jane was about to leave, the hysterical giggle finally escaped from Lexie's lips, sounding like a mouse sucking helium. Jane's head swiveled around, and Lexie jerked back behind the suitcases.

Carpet squish . . . closer . . . Jane was coming closer! Lexie broke into a cold sweat. A banging of metal against metal told her that Jane was inspecting the discarded music box as the source of the noise. More movement, then at last, she heard the front door slam shut again.

She slipped out of her hiding place and retrieved the passport. Inside was a photo ID of Jane E. Lewis. It was a pretty picture. After all, the Bimbo was molded with plastic goop. If you cut her she wouldn't bleed, she would ooze.

Lexie flipped through it, page after—oh my God!—blank pages! This passport had never even left the United States! It was as clean as Jane's suitcases. Skipping back to the ID page, she verified the issue date: three years ago! Hello? Jane was a first-class fake! And here was the proof. As if Lexie needed it. She had known all along that Jane was an Alien in Exile (probably for trafficking in recyclable body parts). If only her dad had listened to her.

The sound of Jane's engine roaring to life sent a shot of adrenaline through Lexie that numbed her backache. She shoved the passport back in place, covered her tracks, and blasted out of the room. As she ran past the living room window, she saw Jane's car backing down the driveway. In a stealthful, all-but-silent move, she opened the front door as Jane drove into the street. Bending low, Lexie dashed over to her bike and sped off in pursuit of the Criminal.

The ground seemed to give way under her laserlike intention. It grabbed her bike's rubber wheels with its asphalt tentacles, sucked them in, and spit them forward. She was flying!

Like an inventor on the verge of a great discovery, she was

operating on sheer instinct. She had bypassed her mindware and was taking direction straight from her own True Source. Recent events flashed on her Inner Screen with the beautiful mathematical precision of a well-ordered series of numbers: Zoe's *Virtual Personality* program, Mom's online visits, Pegasus— Jane's horse *and* a patient code for Susan Butler—and Jane's unused passport. The perfect symmetrical progression of these clues convinced Lexie that she was being led along the path to righteousness and freedom. She humbly thanked the cosmic forces, including her mother.

Ahead, she spotted Jane's Jeep as it sped through an intersection and turned down the next street. Lexie groaned as the light changed to yellow. Could she make it? With lifelong expertise gained by playing zillions of video games, she assessed the situation.

Left cross street: ancient car with old woman driver = slow starter.

Right cross street: station wagon with stressed mother distracted by unruly kids in backseat = unpredictable starter. If kids behave, may start fast.

Summary: Cut to the left.

Decision: Go for it!

Lexie raced through the intersection. *Oops! Miscalculation! Reject! Reject!* A van backed down a driveway, hit a trash can, and then crossed in front of her. As she swerved to avoid being hit, Lexie's pedal lightly scraped the station wagon's front bumper. Her bike wobbled, and she almost fell in the middle of oncoming traffic but managed to regain her balance. Speeding off, she heard the mom yell at her kids, "Look at that crazy girl! Don't you ever, *ever* do that!"

Relieved her casing was still intact, Lexie thanked her lucky stars once more and updated her AUTOMOBILE PROJECTION PATTERN file to include cars driving backward in any analysis.

Turning the corner, she spotted Jane parking in front of a small, run-down bungalow with an anemic lawn and a wheelchair ramp. Lexie hid in the shadows of some jacaranda trees across the street and observed Jane, who opened the gate in the chain-link fence and, with the confidence of a frequent visitor, walked to the front door. Maybe Jane had a secret boyfriend! After all, she couldn't really be in love with Lexie's dad. He wasn't boyfriend material; he was her dad, for God's sake.

Here we go, she thought, watching the door open. But instead of some hunk, she caught sight of a woman about Jane's age in a wheelchair. Through the front picture window, she saw her opponent enter the house and talk to the disabled woman. Then she handed the woman the packet of money from her purse. Jane's agitated gestures told Lexie this was no social call. But what business could Jane have with this poor woman?

Look there: The woman's mailbox was red-hot. Scrunching down low on her bike, Lexie paddled her feet till she was along-side of it. The rusty metal door creaked as she opened it. Inside, she spied a pile of mail addressed to Jane Lewis. *Does Jane live here?* she wondered. But then a catalog advertising hospital-type supplies like wheelchairs and walkers slid out of the mailbox and landed at her feet. It was also addressed to Jane Lewis. Lexie's Internal Analyzer didn't have to compute for long: Jane Lewis was the woman in the wheelchair. But why did these two women have the same name?

The sudden sound of wild barking put her on alert. Her heart leaped at the sight of a rabid Doberman pinscher flying around the side of the house, straight for her. It pounced upon the fence with a loud *Clang!* And there was Jane, peering out of the window at her! For a single, unguarded moment, their eyes locked. Then Jane started out the door. Clutching the revealing catalog, Lexie shot away on her bike like a rocket.

THROUGH THE LONG night and torturous next day at school, Lexie's suspicions about Jane boiled inside of her until she thought she would burst. Not a word, not even a Monitor B impression, however, did she give her dad when their paths crossed at home. This time, she decided, she would deal with a professional.

The school bus had barely come to a halt when she hit the ground and ran home to get her bike. Standing up from the saddle, feet pumping the pedals, she sped through Palisades Park, turning down Colorado Avenue and onto the small bridge over to city hall. Brimming with confidence, she locked her bike in front of the police station and walked up the front steps. As she pulled open the front door, she automatically wiped her hand on the back of her jeans; the thought of absorbing some of the downgraded matter that passed through there every day grossed her out. Inside, an officer at the front desk offered his assistance.

"Detective Blackwell," she said, fixing the man with tractor-beam intention. "I have to see him."

"What about?" the officer said.

"I have important information for him."

He looked her over, and Lexie got a hit from his Monitor B: *Humor her.* He barked into an intercom, calling Blackwell to the front.

"Just wait," he told her, pointing to the lobby.

She studied a bulletin board tacked with pictures of criminals at large, half hoping to see Jane in disguise. Several minutes later, a large, cold hand on her shoulder startled her.

"Looking for me?" a deep voice said.

Lexie turned to find the man she remembered, once more holding the worry beads in his hand. But her courage wilted in the face of his gigantic authority.

"Um . . . ," she said.

"Can I help you, Ms. Diamond?"

Lexie nodded in her peculiar way, marveling at the aptness of his family name. His black eyes were like a deep well that would drown your lies, silencing all but the truth. Well, this was the truth. Even though she hadn't connected all of the wires yet, she had enough clues to point this Alien Catcher in the right direction.

"I know who killed my mom," she said, reminding herself

that there was no reason to fear him; he was just another grown-up.

"But we had a bona fide confession note from Susan Butler," Blackwell said, daring her with his penetrating gaze.

"Well, I've got proof."

Blackwell slid the beads faster, never taking his eyes from her. "C'mon," he said, cocking his head. "Let's see what you got."

He led her down a hallway into a small, fluorescent-lit lunchroom and bought a chocolate ice cream bar out of a vending machine. To her surprise, he handed it to her. He hadn't even asked which ice cream she wanted, or if she wanted one at all! What was this, Standard Operating Kid Procedure? She stared at the inviting treat with reluctance. She wanted it all right, but she was just so fed up with being "fixed."

Grown-ups were always trying to fix her—as if she were broken. It always had to be *their* way. Forget about the tired hand-me-down lives that they expected you to adopt; it was the day-to-day fixing that drove her nuts. With every little decision they fixed you—from picking the stupid ice cream bar to deciding what you could watch on TV. And the sad thing was that one day you woke up totally fixed—a grown-up forever. What was it the adults were so afraid you might become if left to your natural instincts, anyway?

Lexie's stomach growled, reminding her that she had skipped her after-school snack, so she justified accepting the detective's offer. Besides, if she refused, he might become unpre-dictable. At least this way the cop could maintain the illusion that he was in charge. Morphing into a compliant kid, she took a huge bite.

Good. He appeared to be listening.

Lexie began to outline her case against Jane: "My dad's girl-friend, Jane Lewis—red hair, Bambi eyes, Barbie doll type, drives a red Jeep—is the one you're looking for. She's, like, a real wacko, Jekyll and Hyde, for sure. One minute, she's super nice and the next, a killer."

Blackwell stared at her, his face impassive, and slowed the rhythmic pace of the beads to a crawl. Lexie realized he was just pretending to listen. They were not connecting. They were not even in the same universe.

How could you communicate with a fix-it freak, anyway? Perhaps if she did fake talk, like Jane, with a heavy dose of Well, Maybe, I Think, What Do You Think? and Couldn't It Be?, Blackwell might be able to understand. Instead it was way obvi-ous that her straight-on, binary-talk lacked flexibility. Of course! People didn't take you seriously if you were too certain you knew something! A typical example of the backward logic that pervaded prisoner planets like Earth.

Sure enough, the detective lazily thumbed a single bead and said, "There's no motive."

Lexie stared at his beads in an obvious, irritated fashion. "Yes, there is," she said. "Jane probably resented the love my parents shared. She felt my mother was a threat to her relationship with my father. The motive was hate; she hated my mother."

Blackwell shook his head, and Lexie winced at his B-side: *They were divorced, kid; wake up.*

His A-speak was more gentle. "Your father said he was single when your mother died."

Better stick to the facts, Lexie decided. "Look," she said, pulling the hospital supply catalog from her backpack. "This is addressed to Jane Lewis. And I saw my dad's girlfriend at the house of the disabled woman this was sent to. The woman in the wheelchair has to be the real Jane Lewis. My dad's girlfriend is a total fake."

"Maybe your dad's girlfriend ordered the catalog for the woman."

"But all of the woman's mail was addressed to the same person, and this catalog proves that Jane Lewis is disabled."

"She could have been a relative with the same name," Blackwell said, with an impatient glance at his watch.

"I don't think so; they didn't look anything alike. Besides, if Jane is using a fake ID, it would explain why she lies about things. She has to cover her tracks. Like, she says she travels all the time, but her passport is blank!"

Blackwell countered. "Could have lost it, gotten a reissue."

"Listen, Jane has a huge amount of cash! Only criminals have cash. And I saw her give a lot of money to the disabled woman, the real Jane Lewis."

"Tell the IRS," he said, his boredom unmasked.

"But there was something freaky going on between them."

"Freaky?"

This would be harder than Lexie thought. If only she could cast spells on people and make them do exactly what she wanted, life would be so much easier. That's what Jane had done to her father: Look at my pretty face while I reach in and trip your switch. Ha-ha, now you're brain-dead and I'm in control. But even if Lexie had had the moral flexibility to be so ruthless, she would have hated being ornamental.

She stuffed the hospital supply catalog back in her backpack and went back to Basic: "Did you look at the patient code list we gave you?"

Blackwell nodded with classic Lexie imprecision. She rolled her eyes. For God's sake, here she was, like, giving him all these freebies and all he could do was file her under MOTHERLESS GIRL HATES GIRLFRIEND.

She sighed, hoping her disappointment registered with him and then continued, real slow. "It's simple: One of my mom's patients was coded as Pegasus, and Jane once loved a horse named Pegasus."

"So your mom had a patient coded Pegasus and your dad's girlfriend was fond of a horse by the same name. Is that it?"

"No." Lexie wasn't stupid! Only it was hard to pass information from the Beyond to someone in this dimension who relied so heavily on earth's all-pervasive program: *What You See Is What You Get.*

She began again. "The patient listed under Pegasus was actually Susan Butler—"

"Are you sure?" he said, and jammed two beads together at once. "Susan Butler was one of your mom's patients, then."

"That's what the list said."

Lexie's B-message: *See, you missed that one. You might have missed something else, too, Mr. Know-It-All.*

Instead of owning his laziness, however, Blackwell only used it to support his mistaken assumptions: "Since Susan Butler was your mother's patient, not Jane Lewis, and your father met Jane after the accident, it seems unlikely that Jane knew your mother. Like I said, Jane has no motive. Furthermore, it only proves Susan Butler's guilt."

"But my mom's death wasn't accidental," she said.

"How do you know?"

"She told me so."

Even as the words popped out, Lexie realized that she had broken the first rule of the Virtual Believers' Club: *Don't talk about it.* She understood that someone could only be converted by seeing the Light.

A dozen three-foot-tall, monitor-headed, blue-suited members of the Intergalactic Security Patrol capture me within their force field. The leader places a black, stick-on dot over my ajna spot. He telepathically communicates that I will be identified forevermore as a traitor to the Force. I have lost my cyberprotection.

Blackwell squinted one eye. "So when, exactly, did she tell you this—recently?"

Retreat, retreat! "I dunno," she said, showing sudden, intense interest in her ice cream.

But the detective was tracking her. "And just how did she do that? In a dream or perhaps a little voice in your head?"

Lexie peered right into his soulless eyes and threw a guilt bomb at his Childhood Memory Finder, which was covered with all kinds of creepy sludge and disgusting globs of denial.

"It's nothing like that!" she said. "She's trying to help me, unlike some people!" Then, for extra measure, she dumped the rest of her ice cream into a nearby trash bin. She turned to leave with a loud squeak from her Nikes on the linoleum floor.

As she pedaled away, she warned herself to fight off the inevitable Negballs, which she could already feel snaking through her being, with a healthy dose of Posballs. This was no time to second-guess herself. Her mother was depending on her. To defeat Jane, however, Lexie realized she would have to beat the insidious cancer of self-doubt, once and for all. She must build up self-affirming muscles, which were still weak. She summoned her courage and braced herself from spinning out on the dualistic mental roller coaster. It wasn't easy. One by one, she countered each Negball by recalling her mother's visits and all the encouragement she had sent, especially her advice: *Trust yourself.*

I T WAS LATE AFTERNOON, and all Lexie had eaten since lunch was a few bites of Blackwell's kid-fixing ice cream. She was starving now, but the last place she wanted to go was home. She was cycling toward Montana Avenue to pig out at DiDio's, when Zoe blipped onto her screen. She was up ahead, walking a little hairy box of a dog on a leash. Lexie watched as the animal pooped and Zoe scooped it up with a pooper-scooper.

Lexie sighed. A perfect example of the absurdity of Life on Earth: a small furry pet downloaded its waste, then a human goddess pet collected it. The Cosmic Jokers had to find that insane little ritual extremely funny.

As she rode closer, an older man in a cool-looking, vintage Mercedes-Benz with an open top, his bald head shining as brilliantly as the car, pulled up next to Zoe. Lexie could hear him call out.

"Hey, honey!"

The dog barked excitedly and ran toward the car, pulling Zoe with it. The man smiled and stepped out of the car to pat the dog but dropped any trace of adoration when he turned to Zoe. Lexie couldn't hear what he said, but no special sensitivity was required to understand that he liked Zoe as much as Jane liked Lexie.

The man flashed his teeth at the dog once more before he drove off. Lexie thought Zoe looked much smaller than ever before and figured she, too, had been crushed by a pile of Negballs.

"Hey," Zoe said as Lexie glided to a stop.

They looked at each other, each revealing the deep loneliness they shared, like two kindred spirits. The painted, blow-dried curtains hiding the Wizard of Zoe's Oz had parted, and Lexie finally understood that they were alike after all.

The dog growled at Lexie, and she suspected that it had sensed her earlier disgust. Zoe jerked its leash.

"Shut up, Flicka," she said, throwing a murderous look at the cute animal. "This is my Step's real 'daughter.' I was supposed to be at this awesome party—like, everyone is there. But, no-o-o, I have to babysit the hairy princess. How boring!"

Lexie tried to appear sympathetic rather than stunned. She had always assumed that anything Zoe wanted, she got. It was liberating to learn that even charmed lives had dents in them.

"Well, c'mon," Zoe said. "No one's home. Let's kick it."

For a moment, Lexie watched Zoe walk away. It hadn't registered that Zoe had actually invited *her* over. But when Zoe turned around and commanded her to follow, she obeyed, amazed to be hanging with the Popular One—even if Lexie was the only one available.

She followed Zoe's bouncing blond ponytail to her house and parked her bike in the industrial-carpeted garage. While Zoe locked the dog in the laundry room, Lexie scanned the antiseptic house for some sign of life. Her own home displayed evidence of each stage of Lexie's existence: her earliest artistic drawings of martians, as well as dozens of photos of her that, like one huge time-delayed image, showed signs of her developing nerdiness. But these walls were empty, kind of like Zoe, she figured.

The dog whimpered behind the door, but Zoe ignored the pathetic sounds.

"She's such a bitch," she said. "The only peace I get is when she's locked up."

She led Lexie to her room, which was filled with dozens of girl tools: baskets full of makeup, all kinds of spiked brushes and combs, glittery goo pots, machine-gun-style blow dryers, temporary tattoos, stick-on jewels, a rainbow of nail polishes, and many other beauty instruments that Lexie didn't recognize.

"God, I'm exhausted," the Beauty Queen said, slumping onto a faux-leopard-fur-covered bed. "This is my Cinderella gig—work, work, work. I'm just cheap slave labor to them."

Lexie examined a metal scissors-shaped device with flat tonglike heads that resembled a torture instrument, careful not to inflict any damage to herself. "Do you know how to use all this stuff?" she said.

"Yeah, I'm, like, a rocket scientist," Zoe said, dismissing her question.

With a pang, Lexie remembered that she didn't belong there and wondered how to escape. She sank into herself and stared at the vacuum streaks in the carpet, feeling invisible once more.

"Hey, makeup is easy—just, like, one layer after the next," Zoe said, softening her voice. Her Sub-Monitor clearly read: *friend.*

The idea of having a friendship with Zoe both disturbed and fascinated Lexie. It was like coming upon a spaceship that had dropped from the sky. Who knew where it might lead? A real relationship wasn't something you could just click off, either, like an online connection. Things might be expected of Lexie, mysterious things she might not be able to provide. Maybe she would be forced to continue once she had begun, whether she liked it or not. The genuineness in Zoe's eyes, however, persuaded her to let down her force field, at least temporarily, and investigate what a friend was.

"Oh my God!" Zoe said. "I'll give you a makeover."

"Gross!" Lexie said. "You're not putting all that stuff on me!"

"Get real—look at your dad's girlfriend. She's not going to deal with you seriously. You look like a kid! Look at me: three Steps and I'm still living at home, in my own room, instead of in some boring boarding school. Why? Because I never, *ever* let them see that I'm just a kid. Trust me, you've got to be in PMS Mode." Lexie gave her a quizzical look, and Zoe explained: "Prevent Marrying Step."

Could it be that the cybergods had sent Zoe to help her? Could a diva be a clue? If so, Lexie reasoned, shouldn't she go with the flow? Hip to her own logic, she picked up a tube of red lipstick and smeared it across her grinning lips. She looked expectantly at Zoe, who rolled her eyes.

"You are so tragic! Lipstick is last. Everyone knows that—it pulls the whole look together!" They both laughed, though maybe, Lexie realized, not at the same thing. But it didn't matter; she was beginning to understand that Zoe's "attitude" was simply her way of dealing.

"Okay," Lexie said. "I'll make a deal with you: You give me a makeover, and I'll teach you some computer skills." After all, it was a disgrace for the president of the Virtual Club to be totally techno-illiterate.

"Hello? I don't do wires," Zoe said.

"I don't do makeup, either."

It was a standoff until, all at once, they both were overcome

238

with the giggles. When they could speak, Zoe assumed command once more. "All right, girlfriend," she said. "I'll go first."

She held Lexie's chin in a delicate fingertip grip and wiped the mess off her mouth with a pleasant, swishing motion. "First, concealer," she said, all sisterlike. "Then foundation, eye makeup, blush, and last, lipstick! *Très* simple."

Lexie rolled the sequence around in her head, trying to compute Zoe's faceware, but it was illogical to her. She watched, mystified, as Zoe whipped out an endless stream of options. Why did this one go here and that one there? And why the Honey Dew liquid and not the Ivory Bisque? Hello? Where was the program manual? But as Lexie watched a more colorful, almost grown-up version of herself emerge in a brightly lit vanity mirror, she realized there was a kind of logic to this tribal painting. It was a type of camouflage, a shield. At least she figured that's how Zoe used it.

Zoe slid a tube of gummy red goo over Lexie's lips and stepped back with a flourish. "There, look!" she said. "Not bad."

Amazed, Lexie pushed back her hair and studied her masked image. She hardly recognized herself but wasn't sure if that was a good thing or a bad thing. Not wanting to appear ungrateful, she didn't ask. "Wow," was all she said.

In fact, Lexie's system was having difficulty importing the whole makeup thing. Wasn't this just another string being added to her puppetlike existence? Why couldn't anyone just see her for who she was? No one ever really heard what she said, and now she had to paint herself blue, gold, and red just to be seen! What a hassle it was to get grown-ups to use their eyes— their B ones. If only her dad would look, he'd see what a corrupted person Jane was. And then Lexie's skin could breathe.

"Okay, my turn," she said, and then the awful thought: "Do you have a computer?"

"My mom does," Zoe said, dragging Lexie into the family room. She pointed to a sleek computer that sat atop a modern glass desk. Lexie ran her fingers over the computer hardware, impressed.

"She uses it to shop," Zoe added. "Me, I'd rather do the real thing."

"It's much faster online. You can cover the whole world with a few clicks."

"Yeah, but I can't see what it looks like on me, can I?"

Lexie didn't see why that would be an obstacle, but then, she hardly ever looked in the mirror. For the next fifteen minutes she held sway on the finer points of computer programming, the origins of the Internet, and how to choose a screen name, all before turning on the computer. But when she paused to glance at Zoe, she found her reading a fashion magazine.

"Zoe!"

The recalcitrant pupil yawned. "I just can't relate," she said, with no hint of apology.

Lexie was dumbfounded. "How can you relate to inert

beauty objects and not. . . ." Midsentence, she jumped up and ran to Zoe's room.

She could hear Zoe call out, "What's wrong with you?"

Within a few minutes she returned, her arms laden with all kinds of makeup. She dumped the pile on top of the desk and said, "I'm all over this!"

Zoe flipped her hair, clearly annoyed. "What, you nerd?"

Inspired by her friend's built-in features, Lexie had found a connection between Zoe's illusory faceware and the true, natural beauty of Lexie's own computerware. She riffled through the pile of makeup and said, "Concealer first, right?"

Zoe rolled her eyes. "Duh?"

"Okay, just follow the sequence." Lexie's words tumbled out, barely able to keep pace with her thoughts. She grabbed a tube of light skin-colored cream and plunked it on top of the laptop. "Concealer is the hard drive of your system," she said. "It hides all your flaws and makes you look way better than you really do, just like the hard drive, which is the brain of the computer and can think way more logically than you can! Next, foundation!"

Zoe handed her a bottle of Warm Ivory foundation, and Lexie placed it next to the modem connection. She continued, caught up in the invention of makeupware.

"Foundation covers the largest layer, your whole face—just like the modem, or phone, which accesses the Internet and lets you cover hyperterritories. Get it?"

Zoe looked at her as if she had gone insane, and maybe she had, but she was cruising now and couldn't stop. It was as if a big fat clue had smacked her right in the face. She didn't know why, but she knew she'd better ride that wave. Her instincts told her to help Zoe access some level of computer comfort, so she had to program in whatever language Zoe spoke, even one as silly as this.

Zoe put her hands on her hips and said with attitude, "What are you on?"

"I'm *in* PMS Mode," Lexie said. She spotted a small black box of makeup, which she had seen Zoe use on her eyes, and scooped it up. "Pay attention!" she told Zoe, but then hesitated. "Um, eye shadow is next, right?"

Zoe blew the frustrated air out of her lungs. "Oh my God, Lex, of course. What else could it be?"

"Yeah, what else?" Lexie asked herself, for the next e-step eluded her. *Relax and let the answer come.* She booted up the computer, concentrating, and with a subtle glow, the answer arrived.

"I've got it!" she said, matching the box of eye shadow to the screen. "People look into your eyes to see what you're thinking! When you want to know what the computer is thinking, you read its screen, see?"

"Uh-huh." Zoe rocked impatiently on her high heels.

Suspecting a lack of understanding, Lexie elaborated. "Okay, listen, the different programs represent the computer's thought processes and you read them—"

"Okay, okay," Zoe interrupted. "On the screen, eye shadow; I get it."

"All right. Then, blush!" Lexie said, proud to have remembered the proper makeup sequence.

Zoe deliberated over several colorful choices. "It doesn't matter!" Lexie said, shouting now. "It doesn't have to, like, go with anything. It's the concept!"

"Excuse me," Zoe said, arching her graceful back. "But the right color is part of the concept. If it's the wrong color, your whole look is ruined." She placed a small jar of Spring Peach blush into Lexie's hand, adding, "This is the right one."

"Whatever," Lexie said, placing it next to the mouse with a jaunty flip of the wrist. "We still have to connect your mind with the computer's. Just like blush highlights your face, the mouse allows you to highlight anything on the screen by moving the cursor! See how easy it is?"

Zoe smirked. "Aren't you forgetting something, Miss Makeup Master?"

Huh? Lexie ran through the menu for this vanity-driven program: hard drive = concealer; modem = foundation; screen = eye shadow; mouse = blush, keyboard . . . bummer, she had forgotten the keyboard!

She looked at Zoe, who was clearly enjoying her dilemma. Giggling, Zoe waved a silver tube of lipstick in the air. "Remember? Lipstick pulls it all together, d-a-a-rling!"

Lexie took the shiny tube from her friend's hand, as if they were finally surfing together, and continued where Zoe had left off, even imitating her fashionista accent. "Like the keyboard, d-a-a-rling!"

She stood the lipstick upright on the keyboard, where it stayed briefly and then toppled, rolling close to the edge. Zoe jumped forward to catch it. "Got it!"

Lexie smiled. "I knew you would. See, computers are way easy."

"Yeah," Zoe said, with a wild gleam in her eye. "Now I can use my mom's identity and score some really cool stuff shopping online. I wouldn't be arrested for identity theft, would I?"

In slow motion, Zoe's words rolled down her designer blouse and jeans, past her painted toes, onto the tiled floor, and up the metal legs of the desk. They traveled up Lexie's jeans and, like little magic scissors, cut through the spidery veil of confusion in which she had been trapped. As the sticky strands gave way, she suddenly understood what before she had only sensed. She dove into the waters of her mind, which were now as crystal clear and as calm as a lake after a passing storm. Some part of her was aware of Zoe staring at her with concern. But she stayed silently focused within, not even thinking, just allowing her Hard Drive to process all of the data in her JANE file. She trusted that when her calculations were complete, the next inevitable sequence would pop up.

Which it did: "Voluntary identity theft!"

"Actually, my mom will be totally pissed if she finds out," Zoe said.

"No! I mean, Jane! What if she paid someone else to use their identity? I saw her give money to this other woman with the same name. The other Jane Lewis agreed to it, see? Identity theft is hard to trace. Imagine how hard it is when it's voluntary."

"Why would someone sell their identity?"

"Because they're having problems anyway, poor and disabled, or alcoholic—like the woman that supposedly killed my mom! I bet Jane bought her identity, too. That's it! She preys on people who are down on their luck, and then when she's cut and pasted their identity onto hers and has no more need for them, she ejects them."

"Ejects them?"

"Kills them," Lexie said, shaking from the intense charge generated from so many connections. The internal heat melted the makeup, and it dripped down her chin in little Honey Gold globs.

"Wow," Zoe said, wiping Lexie's face with a tissue. "Then who is she?"

"I don't know." Lexie shuddered as she recalled her mother's diagnosis for Susan Butler: paranoid schizophrenic. Only she bet it was Jane masquerading as Susan Butler, whom her mother had treated. In fact, Jane was truly insane! Lexie reeled as her suspicions crystallized. "This means Jane probably killed my mom, too."

"But why?"

"If I'm right, it means she was my mom's patient. Maybe my mom was onto her."

Zoe gasped and, as if retreating to her comfort zone, began to brush her hair with wild strokes. "Well, I saw Jane," she said, "and I can guarantee she hasn't had any work done on her face, so somebody who knew her as Susan should be able to identify her as Jane."

Lexie was so impressed and grateful, she wanted to hug Zoe. Instead she paid her the highest compliment she could think of. "You know, Zo, underneath all that *stuff*, you're, like, smart."

"Of course," Zoe said, with a short, perky stroke of the brush.

"As a matter of fact, I know someone who can identify her and solve this whole thing."

"Perfect. Just get the person to testify."

"Yeah, right," Lexie said with unexplained diffidence. "If I can reach her; she's not always available."

"Oh my God, it's important, she'll understand."

"I hope so."

Lexie signed onto Zoe's mother's computer and logged onto virtualbelievers.com. To her dismay, a sign appeared: CIRCUITS OVERLOADED. TRY AGAIN LATER. A quiet panic gripped her, and she wondered what was happening. Was Ajna-Mac the only one who could deliver her into the Beyond? Or was it her own faith, crippled by years of self-doubt, that kept her from seeing past the subtle veil that she had penetrated and longed to sweep aside once more?

"What's up?" Zoe said, glancing at Lexie's forlorn face.

"Nothing. Just technical difficulties, I hope."

T WILIGHT DESCENDED as Lexie left Zoe's house and cycled home. She squeezed the speed out of her bike as if her feet were propelled by the fast-paced revolutions occurring in her mind. One equation after the next solved itself until she had total confirmation of her instincts. She could see her whole experience like a well-drawn blueprint. Her connection to Zoe had not been a random occurrence. Their divergent paths had crossed for a reason. Computer Wizard meets Ultimate Diva, and Universal Justice is served. It was so elegant that it brought tears to her eyes. And to think that she had been stubborn and narrow-minded in resisting the stream of life, which had carried her to this very place. Yet all along someone or something—some powerful, pervasive *Energy*—had been orchestrating events. Without question, her father was wrong;

life was not a random series of meaningless events.

At her street, Lexie rounded the corner past a raspberry guava hedge when she was startled to see a dark form, inches in front of her, crouched low. She swerved her bike out from under her, aiming to jump free from what she feared would be a nasty crash, but her front wheel caught something—a skateboard. She fell headfirst into Wilson. He caught her in his arms, and they rolled together in a heap into the bushes. Huddled under the rain of the plant's small, red fruit, they stared into each other's eyes, breathlessly.

After what felt like an eternity, he said. "Are you okay?"

Lexie shook her head in that nondefinite way of hers. "You?"

"I'm cool."

Up close, she noticed blond fuzz on Wilson's upper lip and, mesmerized, followed its trail to a patch of soft hairs on his jaw. She felt an impulse to reach out and touch the downy growth but stopped when she caught the strange look in his eye.

"You look, um, different," he said, with a crack in his voice.

"I do?" she said, alarmed. She wiped her sweaty brow and felt the gooey Honey Gold foundation on the back of her hand. She silently cursed Zoe until he said, "Yeah, you look nice."

Wow, she thought, *this tribal mask has real power!* Power to make Wilson's body feel very hot and very close. *Yikes!* She jumped away, hit a branch, and tumbled to the sidewalk. He leaped to his feet with ease and offered his hand.

"Whoa, are you sure you're okay?" he said.

Oh my God, for sure he thought she was a total dork. She scrambled to her feet without his help and glanced at him sideways. He was smiling at her with no confusing head trip or mysterious meaning. It just felt good. He might be simple, but he was nice, she decided. Really nice.

She smiled, too. "Yeah, I'm okay."

"Excellent." He righted her bike and looked it over. "Sweet," he said, walking it to her.

"Thanks. Um, are your wheels okay?"

He scooped up his board, with a cursory examination. "No problem."

For a moment they stood together on the sidewalk caught in a shy silence. Twice he started to talk with "Um," or "Hey," but stopped short. She wondered what he might possibly say, but for once she was clueless. At last she shoved off down the street.

"Bye," she said.

"Later," he said, watching her go.

A few feet away, she glanced over her shoulder and saw him wave. It made her smile the rest of the way home. Perhaps she could enlighten him with the subtle truths of Life in the Bubble. Think again: a surfer? Too much work, she decided.

She glided into her driveway and burst into the kitchen, where she was met by the curious stares of her father and Jane.

"Lexie? You look . . . nice," her father said, squinting his eyes.

"Are you wearing makeup?" Jane said.

Lexie ran to the sink, muttering something about an experiment. She poured some dish soap on a towel when Jane appeared at her side.

"Lexie, don't use that," she said in an urgent whisper. "You'll ruin your skin."

Lexie hesitated. If she ruined her skin, Wilson might never smile at her in that oddly pleasing way again. She flung down the offending dishrag.

"I have something better for you," Jane said. "Come on, I'll show you." Stunned, Lexie watched the Trickster walk down the hall.

"What's wrong?" her father said.

"Um, nothing," she said.

She was dying to tell him her startling theory about Jane, but she had to play it smart. She needed a plan, otherwise she knew he wouldn't listen.

She walked to the guest room and found Jane rummaging through a case as full of cosmetics as Zoe's stash. She didn't recall her mother having a similar treasure trove of beauty objects, but then her mother had had a more natural look than both Zoe and Jane.

Jane held up two bottles: one containing a dewy, pearlized liquid and another with rose-colored liquid inside. She handed

Lexie the dewy stuff and said, "This is a gentle cleansing milk for your skin. It won't cause you to break out like soap can. Afterward, put a dab of this toner on a cotton pad and gently rub it over your face. It minimizes your pores, which is so important at your age." She opened the bottle of toner and handed it to Lexie. "Smell, it's rose water."

Lovely, Lexie thought, using her mother's favorite word for roses. But the stench of Jane's crimes overpowered Lexie's senses.

"You can keep them," Jane told her. "Go ahead, use my bathroom."

"Thanks," Lexie said, terrified and confused by Jane's generosity.

Lexie stepped past her, avoiding any physical contact, and closed the door behind her. She felt the walls of the bathroom fall in on her. She couldn't breathe. Why was Jane still acting like a big sister? Lexie took a deep breath and tried to calm her hands, which were shaking so hard she feared she would drop the cosmetic bottles. *Don't be fooled*, she told herself. This was just one more of Jane's tricks. Maybe these pretty liquids were poisoned.

As I rub the pearly liquid on my face, my skin puckers and blisters, then begins to peel off. A river of blood runs over my exposed facial muscles. I scream loudly, but no sound escapes my lips because my mouth is melting. Jane walks in. Our eyes meet in the bathroom mirror. She throws her head back and laughs with a piercing sound that shreds the remaining skin from my face. It falls into the sink in ugly pink lumps.

Just in case, Lexie washed her face using Jane's own stuff from the cabinet shelf. She tried to slip past the kitchen undetected, but her father stopped her. He cleared his throat with an ominous, loud rumble—the one that signaled a major announcement. She dug her toes into the floor, ready to defend her recent espionage, if necessary.

"Come with me, Lexie," he said.

She trudged after him up the stairs, glad that Jane had stayed behind. As they approached Lexie's room, she wondered if perhaps her father planned on locking her in and grounding her for a few years.

"I made a mistake," he said, holding the door open for her. Lexie held her breath, bewildered. "The minute Ajna-Mac was stolen, I should have bought you a new computer." There on her desk was a brand-new, top-of-the-line Macintosh laptop.

"Wow," she said.

It was not Ajna-Mac, but it was awesome. She began at once to piece her new lifeline together. Her hands greedily caressed the shiny hardware; her fingers danced across the new keyboard. Sleek and powerful, this system was capable of boosting her up to the highest level Beyond! Of course no fancy system could ever replace her old friend. Still, she realized, Ajna-Mac would have wanted her to have access. He would be sad to know she was offline, no longer surfing their old haunts. At least, she decided, she would name her new friend in his honor: Ajna-Mac II.

"Thanks, Dad. It's really cool."

"You know I've always supported your interest in computers," he said. "And I think you've been suffering the past few weeks without an outlet for your hobby."

Dad's Monitor B: *Maybe if you have a great new e-toy to occupy your mind, you'll stop harassing Jane and we can go back to normal.*

Once more, the Universe had delivered the perfect clue via her father, sort of: *a great new e-toy . . . to harass Jane.* Like all great ideas, the perfect plan popped into her head fully formed, as if it had always existed and had only been waiting for Lexie's look-see. She chuckled to herself. Her poor dad—he had no idea what he had done. Well, he would get what he deserved for messing around with the devil.

"I'm glad you like it," her father said, studying her.

Then, fearing her new system might suffer the same fate as Ajna-Mac, she asked him for a key lock on her door. She bet Jane also had been responsible for Ajna-Mac's theft, and Lexie couldn't risk a second occurrence.

"Is that necessary, Lexie?"

With a wink to Karma Kong, she appealed to her dad's Widower With Girl Child vulnerability. "I'm maturing, Dad," she said. It was true, wasn't it?

He reddened slightly. "I understand."

She gave him a big hug, then kicked him out, nicely. She could tell he had more to say, but she stalled him with, "I've got a lot of work to do!" Little did he know how true it was.

She touched her ajna spot and initiated Ajna-Mac II into the ritualistic worship of energy. With deep gratitude, she accessed the computer's full power and dipped once more into the refreshing field of cyberpossibilities. It felt good to be back home. The last time the tingle of the Web beneath her fingertips had felt this good, she must have been one digit old.

She shot off a message to webrider:

i'm back! missed you!

Her quick response was gratifying:

missed you like crazy, diamondstar!

Then she told Ajna-Mac II, *Let's get serious, my friend.* But he emitted no verbal signals, as his predecessor had done, and she hoped they would be compatible.

She grabbed her digital camcorder and ran down to the kitchen, where Jane was filling a cone-shaped clay pot with vegetables and chicken. Assuming a playful air, Lexie focused the camera on her.

"What are you making?" she said.

"I thought we'd have a Moroccan dinner," Jane said.

"Have you been to Morocco?"

"A few times," Jane said, sounding edgy, for no apparent Monitor A reason.

Jane looked everywhere but at the camera. Lexie was relentless, however, and managed to record a clear picture of Jane anyway.

"What's up, diamondstar?" Lexie's father said as he walked in. His voice was matter-of-fact, but Lexie heard the suspicion. Why did he always have to protect *her*?

"I'm making a sort of documentary about my life for my website," Lexie said. "You know—reality, quantum physics, all kinds of stuff—and I thought Jane should be in it, too." In fact, it was an acceptable version of the truth. Karma Kong had nothing on her this time.

"Terrific! Compatibility—I like that," her father said. His knowing smile telegraphed to Jane that the computer had been a wise investment after all. "Do you want to interview me about—?"

She cut him off. "I have stuff on you already." Without further explanation, she ran back to her room.

Back at her desk, she loaded *The Virtual Personality* program onto her new computer and then downloaded the digital images of Jane. As she typed the necessary words, she felt the pain and confusion that had spun around ever since her mom had left. It funneled through her like a violent tornado onto the screen. Finally, she clicked on Edit and waited while Ajna-Mac II flexed his muscles with a soft whirring sound.

Go ahead, she challenged him, *grab all those fake little vowels and consonants that Jane weaves, and spin a web of truth to snare her in!*

"Just a minute, please."

As Lexie waited, she marveled at her earlier efforts to rid herself of Jane. What was she thinking, wearing makeup or stuffing a piece of paper into an old doll's head? That wasn't her. *This* was. She was just like her computer, the same species. It had an excellent hard frame: sturdy, reliable, low maintenance. Same with her: She didn't need a lot of stuff and she could eat anything. Her computer had a first-class brain, it was way logical, and it never believed something that didn't compute. Ditto! In essence, they were like spiritual plankton floating through an ocean of high-frequency waves, naturally absorbing the all-pervasive truth. United in body, mind, and spirit, they followed those subtle clues like signposts to their destiny.

Zoe wanted her to travel the body path. And her dad pushed her to develop her mind. But she was a whole integrated system; no wonder she couldn't play the game their way. How could they expect her to squash herself into one little box with a single puny label? What was she supposed to do with her other parts? She had to let the cosmic force flow through her—all of her.

The Sorcerer signaled that he had completed his task, and Lexie replayed Jane's virtual confession, which she hoped her mother would soon watch. Then she tried to upload the footage onto virtualbelievers.com, but the site was still inaccessible. She clicked on Download Later. If only the connection would slip through and her mother would come to the rescue.

EACH DAY WHEN LEXIE GOT ON THE BUS, Zoe would move over to sit next to her newly anointed favorite: Lexie. Despite Zoe's Bubble-loving ways, she managed to bend the rules to suit her. Lexie admired Zoe's bravery and logged this latest observation in her ZOE file.

"Did you reach your witness yet?" Zoe asked.

"No," Lexie said glumly. "Maybe she's out of town or something."

"She'll turn up. People always do. Just keep trying, and stay in PMS Mode."

"Thanks." Although Lexie appreciated Zoe's concern, her friend's inquiries only highlighted her despair. Access to her mother's site was still blocked, and Lexie was dying to know if her mom had downloaded Jane's virtual confession. By the weekend, her nerves were frayed, and she thought she would implode if something didn't happen soon.

On Saturday, as was her habit, Lexie checked in at her mother's website first thing in the morning. *Damn. Circuits overloaded. Like mother, like daughter.* Lexie watched the screen for some time, willing it to change. Over and over, she visualized the barrier to the otherworldly portal lifting. Intention, persistence, surrender. But the cybergods ignored her, and she wondered if she'd lost her knack. Okay, she told herself as the morning slipped by, just surrender: She'd hang out at the arcade for a while.

She mumbled her way past her father and Jane and cycled off. Halfway there, her new door key, hanging from a necklace, clanked against her handlebars as she bent low on the tenspeed. It took a few clanks to remind her that she'd forgotten to lock her door. *Ugh!* She circled round. She'd never forgive herself if her new e-mate was in danger.

Nearing her house, she spied Jane's Jeep in the driveway, but her dad's car was gone. Golf, probably. In any case, Lexie didn't want to be alone with a murderer. She'd have to be invisible, she decided. She hid her bike in the shrubs and crept inside. Tiptoeing up the stairs, she heard a bizarre grunting sound coming from her mom's bedroom. She rushed to the doorway and watched, horrified, as a pile of her mother's clothing came flying out of the closet and landed in a large brown packing box.

When her mother had died, Lexie had locked the closet

door with her mother's key and placed it in the dresser drawer. She couldn't bear the thought of anyone removing her mother's clothes. Like holy relics, they had touched her mother's soft skin, and her unique scent was locked within their fibers. Now Lexie saw that same key stuck in the open door. In slow motion, reality hit her—someone was trying to erase her mom's image. No one, absolutely no one, had the right!

Lexie raced to the closet. Stunned, she saw Jane rip a handful of dresses from the hangers, as if she wanted to obliterate every trace of Lexie's mother. Oblivious to Lexie's presence, she continued on her rampage, seemingly caught up in a frenzy. When she yanked out Lexie's mother's favorite cream-colored nightgown and began shredding it with her hands, Lexie felt as if the skin on her own face—which so often had been lovingly pressed into that very fabric—was being torn off.

"Stop it!" Lexie cried.

She lunged forward and grabbed Jane by the arm. Jane screamed and spun around, knocking Lexie to the ground. For a second, they stared at each other with all their software exposed. Only this time, Lexie was convinced she saw Jane straight up. She had an awesome view of her Innermost Screen, right into the very depths of her mangled, rotting wiring. There was absolutely no difference between what Lexie saw and what she felt. Jane's A and B Monitors matched! Even her dad wasn't bewitched enough to miss this. But Jane's unexpected laughter jammed Lexie's circuits.

"Oh my goodness!" she said. "You scared me. I thought a bug had landed on me! They're everywhere. We should have cleaned out this closet a long time ago."

Got you! Lexie had just peered into the black hole of Jane's freeze-dried soul, and she wasn't buying the Revised Version that Jane was now selling. Hello? If she imagined this, then *she* was an alien, not Jane! With a righteous look at her torturer, she jumped to her feet and yelled. "You did it!" And she kept yelling until she had cornered Jane in the closet. Then she locked her inside.

"Lexie, let me out!" Jane called out. "There must have been some candy in the pockets!"

"Yeah, right!" Lexie's heart pounded in her chest as she stomped to her room. Her hands shook as she dialed her dad's cell phone number.

"Dad," she said when he answered. "Something terrible happened. Come home quick!"

"Lexie! What's wrong?"

And she knew it was a cruel thing to do, knew Karma Kong would probably triple her negative balance, but she had no choice. It was a matter of life or death. She screamed out loud with all the fury in her heart. It was the cry of someone who wanted to break something, everything, into a million pieces and then smash those into a gadzillion more, until her world turned to dust. *I want my life back!*

Then she hung up.

A cold sweat broke out on her forehead as she imagined her father's panic. She curled up in a ball on her bed and waited. The phone rang again, but she didn't pick it up. It was easier to ignore Jane's cries. Twenty agonizing minutes later, she heard the familiar sound of her father's car pulling into the driveway. She ran to the top of the stairs in time to see her dad running toward her.

"In there," Lexie said, pointing to her mom's old room.

"For God's sake! Are you all right?" he said, grabbing hold of her.

"No!" she said, leading him toward the evidence. "She's been attacking mom's stuff. She had no right!"

"Who?"

"Jane."

"David! Let me out!" Jane said.

Lexie's father turned on Lexie. "What have you done?" he said, rushing toward the closet.

"But, Dad, look what Jane did!" Lexie said, pointing to the box full of violated clothes.

Bingo! Her dad paused, and Lexie celebrated his B-look with a little smirk. His translation: *What the hell! Lexie is right.*

He unlocked the door, and Jane stepped into the room, sending out repeated and adamant B-blips of her innocence. Once more, her scary mask was gone and she had evolved into the sweet, kind girlfriend. Wow, her expert ability to distort her screen was impressive. It made her nearly indestructible.

teenage mother would walk through the door any second. If only Lexie could have talked to that part of her mother, then maybe they would have understood each other better all along.

"I'm sure it won't be for long," Lexie's grandmother said as she laid out fresh linens on the bed.

"I swear I'm not going home unless Jane leaves," Lexie said.

"We're quite happy to have you here, dear, but I'm sure your mother would want you to be at home with your father."

"I can't, Oma."

"I know you feel like that now. Just give it some time."

With a heavy sigh, Lexie placed Ajna-Mac II on top of her mother's old desk. "Whatever," she said.

"Why don't you ask your mother what she thinks? Remember what I told you? I'm sure she'll answer you."

Lexie's eyes teared over, and she avoided her grandmother's gaze. "I don't think so."

"Just give it time," Oma repeated, patting Lexie on the back. "I'll be in the kitchen if you need me." And then she left.

Lexie crumbled, and her tears rained down onto Ajna-Mac II. With fierce determination, she rubbed the computer dry with her sleeve and forced herself to connect with hyperspace. It felt weird to perform her access ritual outside of her own room, but that's what refugees did, she told herself. Although she was only two miles from home, she now inhabited another planet.

She surfed around, played *Vega, The Warrior Goddess*, but nothing could relieve the dull ache in her chest. Some alien had hooked her on its fishing rod, right through the heart, and she would soon be reeled out of this chaotic, polluted fishbowl and eaten as Organic Bubble-Grown Teenager. Why struggle anymore?

Summing up her pain, she wrote to webrider:

> i'm homeless now. staying at my grandparents'
> house. the witch won.

At least her friend understood.

> that sucks.

What else was there to say? Both her parents had abandoned her. *Love dies after all.*

A MONTH PASSED, and Lexie was horrified to realize one afternoon that her stay at her grandparents' house was becoming routine. She had breakfast with her grandparents in the morning and dinner with them in the evening. And every day around four o'clock Oma fixed her an after-school snack: peanut butter and chocolate sauce sandwiched between two graham crackers (a small consolation for leaving home). And every day at that time, her father phoned to speak to Lexie, and each time her grandmother begged her to talk to him, and each time Lexie refused.

Now as she wiped a gooey peanut-butter-chocolate blob from the corner of her mouth onto her T-shirt sleeve, and the despair of her situation engulfed her, she considered that her new habitat might, in fact, be permanent. She might never make it back home ever again. Her father was getting married that weekend. There was no one to stop him, either. There had been no more sightings of her mother online—Lexie didn't even *feel* her around anymore. Her only comfort these days, if you could call it that, was that her Supersensitive Vision had dimmed. Or maybe she just didn't want to look into the Beyond anymore. It was too painful to see anything but the ordinary A-side of life. In effect, she feared she had been broken in, just like all the other pathetic pets in the Bubble.

So when the phone rang as usual that Friday afternoon, Lexie automatically refused to speak. But this time her grandmother hesitated.

"Just a minute," she said into the receiver. Then she covered it with her hand and whispered. "It's Jane. She wants to bring over a bridesmaid dress for you."

Bridesmaid? Lexie made a rapid series of agonized facial contortions, but her grandmother ignored her. "Of course, come on over," she said.

"Oma!" Lexie said as soon as she had hung up. "I'm not talking to her."

"Please make an effort, dear. The wedding is at noon tomorrow. You know your father wants you there."

"I don't care. I'm not going."

She ran out of the house and sped away on her bike. If she had to join the Step Club, she had better start taking instruction from the expert. She pulled into Zoe's driveway and noticed another bicycle leaning against the hedge. Figuring that Zoe had a cool guest, she turned around; then Zoe's dog began barking loudly from inside the house.

Zoe threw the door open, pushed Flicka aside, and called out to her. "Hey, girlfriend, what's up?"

The honorary title soothed Lexie's jangled nerves, and she found herself gravitating back toward the house. "Nothing," she said, rolling her eyes. "She wants me to be a bridesmaid."

"Ugh! That's so not mellow."

Lexie parked her bike and followed Zoe into the living room. Flicka ran ahead, barking at an Asian-American girl whom Lexie recognized as one of Zoe's devotees. The girl was mousing around on Zoe's mother's computer.

"Shut up!" Zoe said, unable to shoo the dog away. "Amy, say hi to Lexie."

Amy and Lexie exchanged nods. "Amy is sort of a geek like you, but a fashion one," Zoe said, with a confessional gleam in her eye. "She's shopping online for me. If my mom finds out, she'll kill me."

"What happened to your tech skills?" Lexie asked, disappointed at her pupil's lack of independence.

"Duh?" Zoe said. "I just had a professional manicure."

Amy grinned. "Can you believe her mom's password is—"

"Her maiden name!" Zoe said, talking over Flicka's mad yelps.

"She even keeps her credit card on file!"

"I bought this awesome pair of boots, and I'm hoping my mom will, like, just think she ordered them and forgot!"

Lexie sat to the side, watching them ooh and aah over footgear. Perhaps she would end up like them. By noon tomorrow her life would be over anyway.

At the pitiful sight of Lexie, Zoe offered to give her a manicure. Without waiting for an answer, she grabbed Lexie's chewed-off nails.

"Chili pepper," Zoe said. "Rub it in every day. Trust me, you'll never bite them again."

"That's disgusting!" Lexie said.

"You nerd," she said with real affection. "Rule Number One in life: You have to suffer to be beautiful." Of course, Lexie's view of beauty was based on internal wiring, but she had no desire to argue with Zoe, who seemed content in her own beliefs.

The consummate beautician handed her a bottle of bright green polish that matched her own painted nails. "This is very in now," she said. Then, once again, she displayed her professional skills as she began to file Lexie's damaged nails with crisp, certain motions.

"It sort of looks like alien pee," Lexie said, examining the bottle.

"You are so weird."

"Thanks, Zo."

"Truly."

Just then, Flicka jumped up onto a chair next to the desk, stuck her wet nose against the computer screen, and barked with increasing passion.

"Help!" Amy said. "Your dog is insane! She's, like, barking at the computer."

With her attention focused on making perfect ovals from Lexie's meager nail tips, Zoe tossed off a reasonable explanation. "She always does that to the computer. It must smell like somebody."

But her innocent words bumped into Lexie's mind with a loud bang, shattering the cocoon of doubt and pity into which she'd burrowed. Up till now, she'd had no confirmation that she wasn't alone in her cybervision of Lost Souls. But dogs had extrasensitive hearing. . . . Perhaps Flicka heard the hum of all that spiritual cybertraffic—*that's* why she was acting so strange! It was enough encouragement to break the crippling spell Lexie had been under ever since she'd left home.

She jumped up, causing Zoe to streak the base coat over her cuticle line.

"You ruined it!" Zoe said, stamping her foot.

Lexie pushed Amy off the keyboard. "Excuse me," she said. "This is an emergency!"

Amy screamed. "Hello? I was in the middle of an order!"

Zoe threw down her tools and grabbed the dog. "It's closet time, sister," she said, carrying her away.

"Stop!" Lexie said, commanding her with such unusual

authority that Zoe obeyed. "I need her! Animals are like sensors, don't you see?"

"What are you on, girlfriend?"

"She's totally strange," Amy said to Zoe.

Lexie tuned out their ranting and, heart beating fast, zipped over to virtualbelievers.com. If she was right—if everything she had ever believed was true—if she really was who she thought she was—that manic fur ball was her next clue. *Maybe Mom is back!* But the voice that greeted her at her mother's website was anything but maternal.

"It's about time!" said a belligerent Lost Soul, floating on the home page.

Lexie gasped. "Who are *you*?"

"I'm number one, I'm first in line!" the old man said, as if Lexie should have known.

"But—" Before Lexie could continue, hundreds of other Lost Souls, all bathed in the incandescent light of the Beyond, crammed onto the screen, creating an unworldly din: "I'm number four hundred and seventy-eight, I'm eight hundred and fourteen, I want a toasted sesame bagel, Where's my new car?, I need to speak to John! . . ." until Lexie feared the address to the heavenly cybergates had been changed to virtualbelievers.com. At the sight of the demanding crowd, Zoe's dog emitted a piercing whine and shied away from the computer. The girls, Lexie noticed, had fallen oddly silent.

"Where's my mother?" Lexie said. "What did you do to her?"

The old man materialized once more in front of the excited crowd of celestial interlopers. "Are you going to help me, or not?" he said. "I've got something important to tell my wife!"

"What? I have to speak to my mother, Grace Diamond. It's urgent!"

"She'll just have to wait her turn."

At that, an authoritative woman, who had the efficient look of a secretary, popped onto the screen and said, "Grace Diamond is number two hundred and forty-seven."

"But this is my website!" Lexie said.

The old man turned to the waiting crowd. "Hey, she thinks she owns this space!"

Bolts of laughter rocked the screen, and Lexie cringed at the intensity. She scanned the confused faces of Zoe and Amy—two ordinary, popular products of the Bubble—for signs of recognition. After all, Flicka's reaction wasn't proof enough. Once and for all, Lexie needed to know if what she saw—not just the images of her mother, but everything that she experienced in her heartfelt interpretation of life—was just a figment of her fertile imagination, or if she had in fact accessed another dimension. There was more at stake now than Lexie's future in Step-hell. Her whole cybersoul was in question.

The girls peered into the screen. After a long, puzzled moment, Amy said, "What kind of virtual personality is this?"

"Yeah, they seem, like, real," Zoe said.

THEY COULD SEE IT! Lexie realized, laughing out loud.

Her heart burst with joy, and she virtually got down on her knees and praised cyberheaven for restoring her faith. She had not imagined any of it: this divine portal, her mother's presence, her clues, or the truths of this crazy world. She *was*, after all.

"Are you going to help us, or not?" the gruff old man said, with increased urgency.

Amy jumped back from the screen and said, "This is *way* interactive!"

Zoe's face had turned a shade whiter and no longer perfectly matched her foundation. "What is this?" she said.

"They're waiting to fulfill their last request so they can be uploaded into a new screen and a new life," Lexie said, matter-of-factly. If they had thought she was weird before, the two girls now looked at Lexie as if she had lost her mind.

"What?" Zoe said.

"You mean, they're, like, dead?" Amy said.

"Serious?"

Lexie nodded. "Serious. Well, sort of. They're still connected. My mom's waiting in line. I've got to get to her."

Amy looked awestruck as she mumbled something to herself in Chinese. "Oh my God," she added, in a reverential whisper. "You found a portal to the ancestors."

"You're kidding?" Zoe said.

"For real," Lexie said. "I actually stumbled onto it thanks to that funky virtual personality CD-ROM you gave me."

Zoe tossed her perfect hair over her shoulder, puffed her

chest out, and once more took charge. "I knew it was special," she said. Lexie was so happy that she resisted the impulse to roll her eyes.

"What do they want us to do?" Amy said.

Lexie shrugged. "Deliver their messages."

Zoe pulled her cell phone from her hip pocket and held her manicured dialing finger in the air. "I'm ready!"

Lexie turned to the gruff old man and said, "What's your wife's phone number?"

As he called it out Zoe dialed. "Tell Louise," he said, "I hid some money in a loose wall panel, behind the kitchen clock. A lot of money."

Zoe signaled that someone had indeed answered. "Um, Louise?" she said, hesitating. She hit the speakerphone, and they heard an old woman's wary voice.

"Yes?"

"What's his name?" Zoe asked Lexie while pointing rudely at the computer.

"Jack!" the old man said. Zoe stared blankly at him, and Lexie felt a warm rush of almost parental pride. Zoe was having her first higher encounter on the Web.

"Get to the point!" Jack said.

Shaken, Zoe spit out his message. But the only response was a heavy silence. The old man leaned into the screen, as if he wanted to reach through the net that separated him from his beloved and reassure her of his presence.

"Sweet Pea! Call her Sweet Pea!" he said.

Zoe rolled her eyes but maintained an earnest tone. "Sweet Pea?"

Loud sobs echoed through the speakerphone, then a shuffling and moving of objects. At last Louise spoke, her voice full of wonder. "It's here!" she said. "There's money in here!"

The cybersecretary announced the next in line. "Number two!"

The old man's face relaxed and he flashed a look of eternal gratitude to Lexie and her friends. "Tell her I'll always love her," he said, then disappeared.

Zoe repeated the tender message, then gently hung up the phone. She turned to Lexie. "What was your mom's number?"

"Two hundred and forty-seven," she said with a sigh.

"Let's rock!"

Zoe and Amy worked the phones while Lexie wrote e-mails. As the night wore on, the trio delivered celestially channeled messages to grateful relatives, children, friends, lovers, business partners, even pets. Flicka, gradually accustomed to the influx of Lost Souls, fell asleep.

After several hours, Lexie noticed that she and her new friends had a gentle glow in their faces, as if they were being wrapped in the starlit warmth of the Beyond. Perhaps, she theorized, these grateful e-folk had showered them with Posballs drawn directly from the ultimate, pure energy source, nullifying their earth-bound Negballs. Maybe once and for all she could break free from the intricate web of doubt and conformity that formed the very walls of human existence and finally trust her own instincts.

At last the woman in charge, frazzled by the hectic pace, called out Lexie's mother's number. Lexie caught her breath as her radiant mom appeared once more, smiling at her.

"How's my Shiny Diamond?" she said.

"Mom! What happened?"

She nodded toward the exhausted secretary, who was resting in a corner. "If it weren't for her, there would still be chaos. Once word got out, every Lost Soul around demanded access to your site. It took some time, but she organized a system based on several ethereal variables; she used to be secretary to a big CEO."

The woman smiled with modest pride and checked what looked like a small handheld computer. "Ten more bytes," she said.

At Lexie's confused look, her mother said, "Time isn't measured in the same way here."

Of course, her mother was outside of Time and no longer subject to its normal progression. "But why didn't my video record you?" Lexie said.

"All you're actually seeing is pure energy," her mother said. "A subliminal imprint of past form is embedded within the energy so you can see it if you really look. But the imprint lacks enough definition to be recorded. And then, of course, as the energy transforms—with upgrades or downgrades—the image gets weaker until at last it fades away."

"Cool." Then she turned her attention to the crisis before them. "What about Jane?"

"I saw your little virtual documentary, you clever girl." Her mother took a deep breath. "It's true, when I knew Jane she was called Susan Butler. The real Susan Butler sold Jane her identity, just as you suspected."

Lexie gasped with relief and horror. Her poor mother. "But why?" she said.

"As her therapist, I was a dangerous link between the past and the present. In order to get her medicine, she needed me, otherwise she couldn't function. At one point I think she even wanted to get better, but once you start down the road to the dark side, it's hard to resist."

The final confirmation of Lexie's suspicions was bittersweet. "I wish you'd never helped her at all," she said.

"Honey, life is like a merry-go-round. Sometimes we get caught up in the problems spinning past. The only thing we can do is try and stay present, in the center of the wheel, detached from the chaos that cycles by, over and over. Help when you can, but never forget that you are simply watching the wheel of life pass by."

"But Dad won't help me. No one believes me."

Just then a small circle of people formed behind Lexie's mother. "I do," one said, then another, until a resounding echo of affirmation filled the cyberhalls of the Beyond.

Her mother acknowledged them. "Jane's trail of tears." She nodded to a forlorn Lost Soul quivering at the edges of the screen. "That's Susan Butler."

"Oh, my God—but what can I do?" Lexie said.

"You've already come further than you ever imagined," her mother said. "At one of the darkest moments in history, a great woman, Eleanor Roosevelt, said: 'Do the thing you think you cannot do.' Lexie, just keep going and let your heart lead you."

Mom was right, Lexie decided. There was no turning back. If only . . .

"Do you think Dad could see you if he really looked?"

Her mother's gaze turned thoughtful. "You never know. Some people spend their whole lives resisting the truth. Some see it in the last moments before they depart. I think your faith is firm enough to be contagious. Just look at them." She nodded toward Zoe and Amy, who waved hello.

It was true. Once upon a time, Lexie would have thought she had been body-snatched by aliens if she'd imagined herself hanging out in the Beyond with the most popular girls in school. And yet it only proved that everyone, no matter what their type of hard frame, operated on the same internal energy.

"By the way," Lexie said with downcast eyes, "there's something I've been meaning to tell you." She pointed at the Diva. "Zoe is actually the president of the Virtual Club."

A flash of surprise glinted in her mother's eyes, but her warmth never wavered. "I understand," she said. "I'm glad she's your friend. Remember—"

Before she could finish, the cybersecretary called for the

next number, and Lexie's mother's image flickered in the brilliant light.

Lexie cried out, "Wait! Mom, you have to come to the wedding, noon tomorrow. It's the only way."

Her mother seemed to fight against a powerful current as she pulled herself back into place. Never losing her sense of propriety, she glanced apologetically at the line of Lost Souls who strained to shuffle forward.

"I'm afraid it might be quite a while before I get another slot," she told Lexie. "That is, if you continue to help these people."

"I won't! I'll close it down unless they let you pass the line." Screw democracy. It was her site.

A communal gasp arose from those gathered in the Beyond. With the kind of disapproval reserved for spoiled children, the secretary ignored Lexie's threats, and tapping her finger against her machine, repeated the next number. An important-looking man in a business suit tried to step around Lexie's mother, but she held firm.

She shook her head in disappointment. "Lexie, this is not your site any more than we can claim our small lives, which we think we own. We are all just passersby in life. That very sense of false ownership is what brings about a feeling of separation and pain."

And keeps the Bubble intact, Lexie realized. Still, she was desperate for control. "But, Mom!"

"I'll try, honey, but it's not up to me," her mother said. "I have to go now. Please be careful." Before Lexie could argue any further, she disappeared into the intangible, but very real, grid of existence.

"No!" Lexie said. *Don't leave.* But she knew she was powerless to stop the tide.

"Let's go," the businessman said, stepping into place.

"I'm serious," Lexie said. "Let my mom in at noon tomorrow, or that's it. Forever."

The man glared at her. "But it's my turn, little girl," he said.

And maybe her problems weren't that important in the whole scheme of things. But right now, she just didn't care.

"Take it or leave it," she said, and shut down the computer.

"Wow," Zoe said, breaking the meditative trance they were under. "You know, Lexie, if you close the site, you won't ever see your mom again, either."

"I know," Lexie said, never taking her eyes from the blank screen. She had come this far; she would have to trust that she was on the right path. *Intention, persistence, surrender.* The last one was a little hard to swallow. "It's a risk I have to take. Let's just hope the Lost Souls realize I'm the only game in town. We'll log on tomorrow, as soon as the wedding has started."

"We?"

"I need your help."

Zoe placed a comforting hand on Lexie's shoulder. "Amy has advanced math tutoring on Saturdays, but I'll be there for you."

"Thanks."

"Ooh," Zoe said with a little squeal. "I'll do black leather with silver stilettos, very secret agent."

"Whatever works," Lexie said, grateful to the omniscient power that had brought her such an unexpected ally. "Just don't be late. Noon sharp at my house, okay?"

"It's a date," Zoe said.

Lexie petted Flicka on her way out and turned at the door to see Zoe and Amy watching her. They looked different, more open, less fake. After all, they had been inducted into that rarest of clubs, the Virtual Believers' Club. They were like sisters; Lexie wasn't alone anymore. It gave her courage to say, "Hey, you guys are for real."

They both smiled. "You, too, Lex," Zoe said. "You're cool."

Lexie waved good-bye and stepped into the dark night. As she rode her bike back toward Oma's house, she played on her Internal Screen several possible endings to the Jane Game. Even if all the e-powers were on her side, she was up against nearly insurmountable odds.

It was a long shot, but one more option remained. With a knot in her throat she called the police station from her cell phone. Although it was late, maybe Blackwell would still be in—crime never stopped. He wasn't, but she could leave a message. She racked her mind to summarize the situation as the detective's machine signaled her to begin.

"This is Lexie Diamond. I know you think I'm nuts, but here's the truth: My dad's girlfriend paid Susan Butler and then Jane Lewis to borrow their identities. You were tricked; it was *voluntary identity theft.*" She repeated the label twice before continuing. "Once my dad's girlfriend switched identities, she killed Susan Butler, so her next victim will probably be the real Jane Lewis, or maybe even my dad. It will be *your* fault if she kills again. My dad is marrying her at noon tomorrow—please do something!" She hung up. At least her message would appeal to his colossal pride.

As her mother had said, she would just have to keep going. Tomorrow would be the ultimate test.

L EXIE WOKE WITH a shock. Today was the day. She
glanced at her alarm clock and cursed her teenage growth
hormones—she'd overslept. Her father's wedding was only
an hour away! A light knock on the door startled her.

"Lexie?" her grandmother said. "Are you all right?"

Lexie jumped out of bed. "Oma!" she said, flinging open the
door. "We're going to be late for the wedding."

Her grandmother hesitated, surprised. Despite Lexie's earlier adamant refusal to attend the ceremony, Oma switched gears
with little apparent effort—no judgment, no questions, no com-
ment. Her grandmother never tried to "fix" her, and Lexie loved
her for that.

"All right, dear. Just a minute, come with me."

Lexie followed her down the hall, watching her soft body

moving one part at a time. Her grandmother lifted from the closet a garment wrapped in clear plastic, along with a shopping bag on the hanger, and gave it to Lexie.

"What's this?" Lexie said.

"It's your bridesmaid outfit, of course," her grandmother said, heading toward her room. "You better get dressed."

No way! Lexie had never agreed to *help* Jane marry her father. She ran to her room and stuffed the articles in the wastebasket. But as she pulled on her jeans, she reconsidered. The closer she could get to Jane, the easier it might be to stop her. *Ugh!* She retrieved the dress from the trash, ripped off the covering, and examined it more closely: high-neck, knee-length, pink satin with a cream-colored, ruffled lace collar. Only Jane would dream up this instrument of alien torture. Lexie pulled the offensive body wrapper over her head and shuddered as the scratchy lining slid against her skin. How was she supposed to go into mortal combat dressed like a useless doll?

Inside the shopping bag, she found a pair of matching shoes. *Mary Janes?* Vega, The Warrior Goddess, would never go into battle without her knee-high, black leather, lug-soled, scrunch-an-alien boots. Lexie threw away the dainty shoes and whipped on her favorite pair of worn Nikes. It was only a small act of rebellion, but it boosted her courage to face the rest of the day.

Then with hardly a minute to spare, and fearing it might be her last message to webrider, she sent a formal e-mail:

dear webrider,

in case you don't hear from me again, i want you to
know how much you mean to me. if i survive my
dad's wedding today, i really hope that we can
hook up offline.

your true friend,

diamondstar

As she hit Send, she vowed: *If I survive the final showdown,
I'll meet my friend, no matter where it takes me, no matter what it
costs.* Friendship, she decided, was what made the whole world-
wide mess worthwhile.

With that thought, she sprang into action: She unhooked
her computer, piled up the pieces along with her camcorder, and
loaded them into the car. Her grandparents hurried out of the
front door, and they sped off, a tense silence over them.

As they turned down Lexie's street, they passed Wilson skat-
ing in the same direction, surfboard under one arm, the muscles in
his bare chest flexed. Lexie turned to watch him, aching to see him
smile at her once more with that sweet look on his face. For a second their eyes met. It was just a glance, but Lexie suddenly felt
seen. It was as if he had looked right through her and really seen
her. In that moment, their differences felt so unimportant—Lexie,
the gearhead, Wilson, the surfer dude. As the distance between
them grew, Lexie followed his gaze. He wasn't smiling, but there
was an unmistakable yearning on his face. Lexie sat back in the
car. If only she would live long enough to know him better.

Lexie's grandfather drove up her driveway and handed the car over to the valet parking staff. Lexie quickly gathered up her gear. As she ventured into her house, she spotted her father in a dorky penguin tuxedo giving directions to several harried party helpers.

"Lexie!" he said at the sight of her. A big smile burst across his face, and he rushed to her side. But as he registered her load, she could see his joy flip to suspicion. He kissed her on the cheek. "Honey, you have no idea how happy I am to see you. But what's all this?"

Intent on faking out Karma Kong's sensors—there was no choice but to lie!—Lexie pasted on an innocent little-girl smile. "It's my wedding present to you and Jane," she said in an overly bright tone. "I'm going to webcast your wedding."

Her father studied her for a moment, unconvinced. "Who would want to see our wedding?"

"Are you kidding? People watch totally boring stuff online all the time. Besides, you'll have an awesome record of this unbelievable day!"

To her relief, her father clicked off the suspicion. "I'm sure Jane will love it," he said, checking his watch. "Just hurry— we're starting soon." Then he strode off, barking more orders.

Lexie set her equipment on top of the patio bar and gazed in disbelief at the backyard, which had been converted into a sugar-coated fairy-tale setting. Rows of miniature icicle lights twinkled from every window and tree and along the edges of a large white tent that billowed over the lawn. A narrow red carpet—the dreaded walkway that Jane would take to marry Lexie's father— separated two sections of cushioned folding chairs. Like a dragon's fiery tongue that would consume Lexie, the carpet rolled out from between the patio doors, ending beneath a vine-covered arch.

Lexie couldn't imagine her father and Jane getting married in this "happily ever after" setting. It couldn't *actually* be her dad's wedding day—it all seemed so surreal, like a reality TV show, *The Wedding*. For weeks this day had been looming, but she had never really believed it would happen. Was this how death came? You knew it would happen one day, but you never really, *really* thought it would. You always imagined that you would be a child forever, that your parents would always be there for you, and that you would always have your same old room.

At the end of a buffet table nearby, a grotesque cake of cascading pink roses towered four feet in the air. Lexie's eyes traveled past each layer to the top of the confectionary monstrosity where bride and groom dolls hovered in a sea of icing! *Smash it to smithereens!* Only the absolute certainty of immediate banishment restrained her from kicking it over.

Time was running out. Already the guest seats were full. With nimble fingers, she hooked up her equipment. Ready for blastoff! But where was Zoe? It was still a few minutes before noon, she consoled herself. Divas were always late, weren't they?

A sudden ripple of oohs and aahs from inside the house drew her to see what the commotion was. Jane, in full bridal gear, appeared triumphant at the bottom of the stairs. She swished toward Lexie, her bridal bouquet cutting through the air as if it were a sword with which she would chop her into little pieces: a telling view of Lexie's Snow White future.

"Hello, Lexie," Jane said, all sweetness and light. "I'm glad you're here."

Her father reappeared at Lexie's side and, with a dreamy look at Jane, said, "Shall we begin?"

"Not yet!" Lexie said, near hysteria. "It's not even twelve o'clock!"

"Lexie," her father began, when Zoe sashayed up to them, wearing a clingy, black thing.

"I'm ready," she said.

"For what?" Lexie's father said, once more suspicious. But a frantic caterer rushed up and occupied his and Jane's attention.

"Love the shoes," Zoe said, checking out Lexie's outfit.

"It's my warrior look," Lexie said.

"Fabulous."

Lexie leaned to whisper in Zoe's ear. "Just remember, as soon as Jane walks up the aisle, log onto virtualbelievers.com. Okay?"

Zoe didn't bristle at being given orders by an underling; she understood how high the stakes were. "Got it," she said. Then as they watched Lexie's father escort Jane to her place at the beginning of the red carpet, Zoe offered her expert opinion: "She is so *not* pregnant."

Lexie blinked hard. "Really?"

"Trust me: Right after the wedding, she'll say it was a false alarm."

"It figures," Lexie said, full of disgust. After all, she had complete faith in Zoe's feminine insights. Her face darkened at the sight of her father striding toward her, and she pointed Zoe toward the patio.

"My computer is over there," she said.

Without a word, Lexie's father took her by the arm and led her toward Jane. Over her shoulder, she saw Zoe examine the equipment and then throw up her hands in bewilderment. Lexie called back to her.

"You can do it, Zoe. You're the president of the Virtual Club!"

Her father snapped to attention. "Can do what?" he said. "I thought *you* were the president of that club."

Lexie sighed. How could Dad pay such close attention to such trivial stuff and still miss the totally major crimes that Jane perpetrated? His mind had definitely been damaged by the warped, upside-down effect that converted kids into grown-ups.

"Well, I'm, like, the *virtual* president," she said, "and Zoe is the real Virtual President, see?"

"Uh-huh," her father replied, the way grown-ups auto-talked when they were no longer listening. Once again he was mesmerized by Jane. Out of her father's sight line, Lexie curled her upper lip into a snarl, but Jane ignored her.

"Special delivery: the maid of honor," Lexie's father said. "Take her, she's all yours." Then he gave Lexie a gentle push, sending her into Jane's waiting cold hands, which tightened around her shoulders like two metallic tongs.

"I've been waiting for her," Jane said, her B-attitude already victorious.

Lexie twisted away from Jane's unyielding grasp and watched her father walk away across the patio. At the end of the red carpet, underneath the vine-covered arch, a Rent-a-Holy waited. Panic gripped Lexie as her father took his place next to him. She stepped outdoors to check on Zoe but was yanked back so fast, her head spun from the g-force.

"You're not going anywhere!" Jane said in an otherworldly voice. "I need you right here."

Her audio sounded part human and part machine; it both terrorized and fascinated Lexie. She turned, suspecting she was about to come face-to-face with her first extraterrestrial, but Jane had already reassembled her perky mask.

"I wouldn't want you to miss anything," she said, with a disarming smile.

Just then a woman led a small child, dressed as a flower girl, to stand in front of Lexie. The doting mother fussed with the girl's hair, encouraged her, then politely excused herself, and sat on the side reserved for the bride's guests. Lexie's Internal

Conflict Catcher immediately told her something was out of whack. She replayed the scene. Oh, but it was so clear: Neither the woman nor the child had said hello to the Bride. Jane hadn't acknowledged them, either. Conclusion: These two "friends" had been hired for the day. Ditto for the rest of Jane's so-called guests. Of course, with all her identity-hopping, whom would she invite?

The notes of the "Wedding March" suddenly reverberated from an electric piano outside, striking an alarm in Lexie's heart. *This was it!* Her knees weakened as she watched the flower girl begin her performance. With each well-practiced, measured step the child took—heel, toe, heel, toe—Lexie felt her anxiety deepen. Her future hung on a delicate thread. Closing her eyes, she silently prayed that the Ultimate Power Source would direct some helpful energy her way.

The next thing she knew, she was being pushed forward and landed with a jerk just outside the patio doors. Behind her, she saw Jane smiling at her. In front, the guests, including Jane's hired friends, waited in anticipation for her to walk past. Up ahead, at the end of the frightful walkway, stood her father. And to her side, there was Ajna Mac II with Zoe next to him, filing her nails, again. *Great,* thought Lexie, *my e-lifeline is in the hands of a techno-challenged princess.*

She lurched one step forward, then another. Her father beckoned her with a slight nod, commanding her with all the power of the life force with which he had conceived her and through which they were still connected. She felt herself drawn to him, as if he were pulling her forward on an invisible cord. She tried to resist, bracing her Nikes against the gravitational pull of her heritage, but the wedding arch came closer and closer until, finally, it loomed like a noose over her head.

As soon as Lexie was across from him, her father released his attention from her and shifted it to Jane. Lexie stood there reeling. For a brief moment, her father had given her his full attention, and she felt dizzy from its abrupt withdrawal. Why had her father stopped looking at her like she was the most wonderful person in the world? What had she done wrong? She suddenly remembered the long-ago sound of his loving voice, which had caressed her like a soft, worn blanket when she was small. She had presented him with a small plastic cup of dripping wet, black mud. "I made it for you, Daddy," her small voice echoed. Her old father, the one she loved best, came into view, smiling as he playfully "drank" her yummy, delicious coffee. "Good java, Little Diamond," he had said. Why wasn't she a good little java maker anymore?

Like a bell from hell, the pianist pounded out the Bride's walking cue: *dum, dum, da, dum*, and Jane began her triumphant march. Lexie craned her neck toward the computer screen. *Not a Lost Soul in sight.* Where in the cyberworld was her mother?

Two more steps and then Jane stood between Lexie and her father. Lexie flinched as Jane attempted to pass off her deadly bouquet. Jane shrugged—she had won anyway—and dropped it in someone's lap.

"Friends, we are gathered here today to join together this man and this woman," the minister said.

Lexie looked for Zoe. There, motioning wildly to her on top of a barstool, was her confused friend. Lexie narrowed her eyes, attempting to read Zoe's lips, which were moving like a puffer fish.

"How-do-you-move-the-arrow?" she lip-synced.

Oh no! Lexie groaned. Which makeup component corresponded to the mouse? Was it the blush or the lipstick? *Think! The mouse, the mouse!* she ranted to herself. Why hadn't Mr. Macintosh put directions somewhere, or was that, like, too obvious or what? She was seconds away from disaster! *Okay, chill! Zen out! Detach! Visualize!*

She took a deep breath and let her thoughts flow: Mouse moves the cursor, so you can highlight the screen; lipstick highlights, no, lipstick pulls it together—try the blush! She moved into the center of the carpet, where she had a better view of Zoe, and with a sweeping motion, pantomimed stroking her cheeks with powder. Her accomplice seemed to understand; she jumped off the chair, and Lexie hoped she'd given her the right direction.

Lexie's father's annoyed cough caught her attention, and she was embarrassed to find everyone looking at her. With a sheepish grin, she shuffled back into place.

The minister continued. "If anyone here has a reason why

these two should not be married, let him speak now or forever hold his peace." Both Lexie's dad and Jane turned at the exact moment, like puppets swiveling on their strings, to give Lexie a warning glance. If it hadn't been so tragic, it would have made her laugh.

After a subtle nod from Lexie's father, the man went on. "Do you, Jane Ann Lewis, take David Alexander Diamond to be your lawfully wedded husband?"

"I do!" Jane said.

Lexie broke into a cold sweat. If her star-tripping cavalry didn't arrive soon, her father would soon be married to this monster.

A NUMBNESS CREPT through Lexie's body, and she yielded to the lethargic ache of whateveritis. What did she care if her father ruined his life? Let him do his thing, and she would do hers. She hadn't asked to be his daughter. She hadn't even asked to be born. He didn't owe her a thing. She stared down at her feet—he hadn't even complained about her Nikes!

"And do you, David Alexander Diamond, take Jane Ann Lewis—"

Lexie held her breath as a high-pitched, electronic roar pierced the air. The minister paused, and the wedding party looked toward its origin: Ajna-Mac II. There, on the screen, shining in the divine cyberlight, was Lexie's mom. Fanned behind her stood an angry rabble of Lost Souls.

One of the Lost Souls pointed to Jane and yelled out, "There she is!" At that, a tumult of insults rose forth from the screen as each accosted Jane by the name they had known her.

Like a balloon losing air, Jane urged Lexie's father in a deflated voice. "Please, do something. Lexie is trying to ruin the happiest day of my life."

"Are you crazy?" he said to Lexie, cutting her a harsh look.

He shouldered down the carpet, but Lexie was faster and ran past him. She barred him from reaching her computer.

"Dad! Just listen."

He spit out his anger. "Damn it, Lexie! How could you do this on my wedding day?"

With righteous fury, he pushed past her, and she fell against the bar. Zoe screamed and, to Lexie's chagrin, crouched behind the computer. So much for her well-dressed accomplice.

Lexie's mother cried out, "David, stop!"

He hesitated. "Grace?" He looked from the computer to Lexie and back again. "Impossible."

"For real!" Lexie said.

He reached to disconnect Ajna-Mac II's electric plug when Lexie's mother spoke in a voice Lexie had never heard. It had a playful, frisky ring.

"Hey, Tiger, it's me," she said.

At once, he froze, then slowly turned toward the screen. His face flushed red, as a kaleidoscope of emotions swept through him.

"Kitten?" he said.

"Yeah," she said with a silly grin.

Tiger and kitten? Lexie didn't even want to know about it.

Her parents stared at each other, and Lexie could see her father's resistance melt as a sweet smile crept across his face. Tears filled his eyes. And her mother's, too.

Then as if Lexie's faith had rippled through the guests like dominoes falling in rapid succession, they began to murmur, and their eyes gleamed with wonder. A tingling current of rarefied energy electrified the air, casting a sparkling luster upon all except Jane.

She bustled down the carpet toward Lexie's father. "It's a trick, David!" she said. "Turn it off!"

His eyes stayed fixed on Lexie's mother. "No," he said, his wonderment in sharp contrast to Jane's panic. "It's some kind of miracle."

Jane stepped in front of him, blocking his view of the screen. "I insist you stop this nonsense!" she told him.

Lexie could almost see Jane's spell take hold of him once more. But he had already been touched by the Light, and he struggled against her control. With a firm hand, he drew her away from the computer. And for a moment, his look ping-ponged back and forth between her and the screen.

Lexie's mother said the words that released him from the spin he was in: "Standing behind me are Jane's victims. I was one, too."

He looked at Jane, as if seeing her for the first time. "Jane?" he said.

"Sweetheart, you know me," she said, a steely coldness betraying her voice. "This is crazy."

The Lost Souls seized the moment and unleashed their suffering in a tidal wave of accusations against Jane. With passionate cries, their voices rang out for justice.

Lexie's father stood still, transfixed by the terrifying display in the Beyond. Even Jane turned as white as her dress.

Through the cacophonous din, Lexie's mother's voice could be heard: "Listen to your heart, David! You know what's true."

"Lies, all lies!" Jane said, floundering. "I'm innocent! Don't you believe me?"

The truth was undeniable. Lexie's father shook his head in dismay. With a loud sob, Jane fled into the house.

"I'll call the police," Lexie said. Lexie's father nodded and slumped onto a barstool next to Lexie's mother.

"I'm sorry for everything," Lexie's mother said to him.

"Me, too."

"Is Detective Blackwell there?" Lexie said into her cell phone. But the next words stuck in her throat, and with horror, she realized Jane had her in a choke hold.

"Put it down," Jane said with total command.

Lexie felt something hard pressed against her back. The phone slid from her hand, clattering to the ground.

Lexie's mother cried out, "No!"

At that, Jane seemed to splinter like a termite-infested house, and her evil self was revealed with such an amazing, volcanic display that the crowd on both sides of the Beyond gasped. With a contorted face and apoplectic rage worthy of a cartoon villain, she cursed Lexie and her parents.

Lexie's father stepped forward to save Lexie, but Jane had the upper hand. She flashed a gun at him.

"Stay away!" Jane barked.

He stopped in his tracks. "All right," he said with false calm. "For God's sake, don't hurt her."

Jane dragged her backward through the yard toward the side gate. Lexie struggled to free herself, but she was no match for Jane's killer grip. Little black dots swam before her eyes, and her heart thumped like mad.

If only she could do something. But her strength was ebbing away, and soon she was too weak to fight. She looked to her mother and father. *Help!* But one was beyond reach, the other unable to move.

The sudden, loud squeak of the back gate opening caused Jane to stumble. There was the sound of hurried movements, a harsh voice. *Blackwell had come!*

He pointed a gun at Jane. "Drop it!" he told her.

Lexie could feel Jane's hysteria rise like a tide that would sink them both. As the seconds ticked by, Jane's breath came in rapid bursts on Lexie's neck, and the sound of her teeth gnashing in Lexie's ear was like a horde of wasps' beating wings.

Jane angled the gun in the detective's direction, while Lexie saw her father gain a few feet. Jane swung back toward him with a second ominous warning. "Stay back, I said."

They were closing in on Jane, and Lexie feared she'd be the sacrifice. *Do something!*

Jane stalled near the buffet table, and Lexie caught her mother's urgent glance toward the long, silver cake knife. Lexie's arm snaked out, and like a blind person fumbling around an unfamiliar corner, she reached for it. Something smooth and metallic was in her hand. *Got it!* She wielded the knife above her, catching Jane's hair. For an instant, Jane was thrown off guard. Lexie's father sprinted toward them. Blackwell came running from the other side.

Bang! Lexie reeled from the explosion. She shut her eyes, afraid to look. All at once she was thrown forward—a human block in her father's direction! *He was all right!* He caught her in his arms and drew her out of harm's way.

She saw Blackwell crumpled on the ground. Jane flew past him, out the back gate, and into the alleyway. Valet helpers shouted, and the engine roar and tire-peel of a stolen car followed. Jane was gone.

Blackwell held his hand over a wound in his leg and struggled for his radio. He called for backup, but Lexie doubted they'd ever catch Jane. Only someone with X-ray Bubble Vision would be able to see through her.

In a daze, Lexie watched her father help Blackwell. Familiar, comforting arms wrapped her in a blanket. *Oma and Poppa.* From somewhere outside of herself, she watched as her grandparents led her toward the house. She was conscious of rubbery legs, guests staring, sirens in the distance, but nothing felt real; her body belonged to someone else. Having journeyed so far beyond the Bubble, she wondered if she would ever feel like a semi-normal kid again.

And then the dam that she had built over the last year to shore up her fragile self broke, releasing a river of tears. Great sobs shook her. She was safe now, and so was her father. It was a bitter victory, though; nothing would bring back her mother.

Lexie's father rushed back to her side. Or was it a shadow of himself? He looked so fragile.

"I'm sorry, Lexie," he said. His apology wouldn't change the way things were, but it soothed the ache in her.

"Are you okay?" she asked.

He looked at her, but she was aware that he was seeing past her, as if there might be a reason to explain the madness. He drew in his breath to say something, then choked on the words. He hung his head on his chest. All she could do was stand very still beside him, her hand in his. After a few minutes, he wiped his tearstained face on his sleeve and hugged her close.

"The important thing is that you're okay," he said in a ragged voice. "That's all that matters. I love you so much, Lexie."

"I love you, too, Dad." In the hollow of his arms she heard

her mother's urgent cry. "Quick—Mom!" Lexie said, running to her computer.

Her mother looked strained. The luminous light shone through her with increasing strength, claiming her wavering image. "I fought the current as long as I could," she said, with tears in her eyes. "I have to go now, sweetheart." Her eyes fell upon Lexie's father and grandparents, who gathered behind Lexie. "Take care of each other," she said.

"We will, I promise," Lexie's father said.

As the relentless tide of life carried Lexie's mother farther into the Beyond, Oma grew pale and leaned into Lexie's grandfather. Her own life force was dwindling as some intrinsic part of her also was being swept away. "Good-bye, dear," she said to her daughter in a shaky voice. "We shall miss you."

Lexie's mother smiled; her love penetrated the whirling forces that gathered speed around her. "Me, too," she said.

Lexie felt the invisible cord that connected her and her mother stretching out across life's Invisible Divide. *Love never dies.* She knew that their connection would never end, but she wanted her little space in the Web to remain as close as possible to her mother's.

"Mom, don't go!"

"Don't worry, we'll always be together."

"Yeah, but . . ."

"You know how to reach me if you need me. I'm right here."

Lexie lightly touched the computer screen. "I love you, Mom."

"I love you, too, Shiny Diamond."

And then her mother disappeared into the cosmic mist.

PING! The shift of the computer gears startled Lexie. With deep gratitude she shut down the computer, and the screen darkened, as if a curtain had drawn closed. She wandered off by herself and sat on a patio chair. As the aftermath of the event swirled around her, she stared at nothing in particular. She simply felt the stream of life circling around her: the tall trees protecting her; the firm ground giving support; soft, clean air nourishing her; sunlight full of warmth and hope. The physical world seemed somehow more inviting, and *real*.

Surrendering to it all, the tangible and the intangible, Lexie was lulled once more into that still center spot at her core. *Here* she would always be able to connect with her mother. And here, in the present moment, she had complete access to her True Self. If she could stay centered, she knew the weight of the past would be nullified and all her power would naturally unfold in sync with the Universal Plan.

In fact tomorrow, she realized, today would be just a memory. Even this moment was already past. But whenever she remembered something, didn't it exist once more in the present? Then *everything* must be experienced in the present . . . and the past, therefore, didn't really exist. If everything except for this present moment was a virtual reality, then whenever she would think of her mother, they would be together again—which meant her mom had never really left.

And until they met again, Lexie knew she would no longer be alone or powerless. With total clarity, she understood that the part of herself that had always been watching the other parts—the unchangeable essence—was connected to the whole web of life. This was her True Self. Her identity as Lexie was, in fact, just a wisp of nothingness, a speck of dust in a great, big universe, as she had always thought. This little part of her was as fleeting as the last blossoms of summer. But her True Self was vast, eternal, and connected to All That Is. There was great freedom in finding her relationship to the whole. And joy.

A loud, commanding voice broke through her reverie, ordering the crowd to move aside. As people scrambled out of the way, Lexie saw ambulance workers carrying Detective Blackwell on a stretcher. His eyes, still penetrating despite his defeat, met Lexie's as he was carried past her, and he saluted her like a comrade.

It was her just due, but—hey, she had had lots of help. With a nod, she acknowledged his praise. A brief smile lit the detective's face, the first Lexie had seen. *Maybe*, she thought, *there is someone home behind those dull eyes after all.*

The befuddled guests swallowed his trail and trudged past Lexie, speaking in low, anxious voices. Soon, she realized, the incident would be forgotten, at least on the superficial A-level. The Bubble's attractions, like flashing lights at a carnival, would soon bedazzle them once more, and all that would remain of their encounter with the Beyond would be a dim awareness of the truth. Only some would dare to remember—hard-core self-programmers like herself.

One thing became clear: If she was to remain free of the numbing effect of the Bubble, truly independent, she must never, ever again doubt herself. She closed her eyes in an effort to hardwire this truth into her innermost programming. Her focus was so intense that she hardly felt the tap at her shoulder.

"Lexie?" someone said. She turned to find Wilson staring at her.

"Wilson. . . ? What are you doing here?"

"I heard gunshots and you know, I was worried. Are you okay?"

"I am now," Lexie said, touched by his concern.

There was a strange pause, and Lexie had the feeling he had something important to tell her. But he could only stammer. "Um." He looked down at the ground. "You said, I mean, well, I thought. . . ."

Then he smiled that smile, and Lexie found herself smiling back. Why, she wondered, did he always make her feel better?

He tried again. "You said in your e-mail that you wanted to meet offline."

Lexie felt her world turn upside down. *Could it be?*

"webrider?" she said.

Wilson nodded. "Hi, diamondstar."

They were connected, had been for years. Wilson, her

cybertwin, was the computer-obsessed geeky girl she had always pictured. It was too absurd, but wonderful, to believe. She burst into laughter, and soon they were laughing together, just as they had so many times before online.

"How did you know?" Lexie said finally.

"I saw your photo on your mom's website, remember?"

"Oh, yeah."

Lexie felt herself flush with embarrassment as she recalled the intimacy they had shared over the years. He knew her better than anyone, except her mom. But he was Wilson, a guy, a simple surfer dude. Then again, nothing was the way it seemed; that's how it was in the Bubble. To discover the truth, you had to look behind the veil of illusion.

Wilson brushed his hand over hers, and Lexie felt an exciting tingle, way more powerful than any e-contact. They leaned toward each other, as if pulled by some irresistible force, and stared into each other's eyes. And they might have stayed like that a long time if Zoe hadn't bounced over to them. At the sound of her voice, they jumped apart.

"Oh my God, girlfriend!" she said. "You should be, like, class president. Hey, come shopping with me." She cast a covetous glance at Lexie's shoes. "I want a pair of Nikes like yours."

"What for?" Lexie said.

"Are you kidding? Next time we help those crazy Lost Souls, I'll be ready."

Yet again, Lexie was stunned by the depth of wisdom that

could come through this committed shopper. Of course, the portal must stay open. For a moment, however, all that responsibility weighed heavily on her shoulders.

"That's a lot of work," she said. "I mean, there's an endless stream."

"Of what?" Wilson said.

"People lost in cyberspace looking for a connection."

Wilson took her hand in his. "No problem, I'll hang with you," he said. And Lexie knew he meant it.

"Me, too," Zoe said. "I'm way into computers now."

Why not? After all, Zoe had proved herself to be a true friend. And Wilson, well, he and Lexie were already virtually inseparable.

"All right," Lexie said.

Hey, she might even learn to enjoy living in the Bubble.